Dear Reader,

Harlequin is celebrating its sixtieth anniversary in 2009 with an entire year's worth of special programs showcasing the talent and variety that have made us the world's leading romance publisher.

With this collection of vintage novels, we are thrilled to be able to journey with you to the roots of our success: six books that hark back to the very earliest days of our history, when the fare was decidedly adventurous, often mysterious and full of passion—1950s-style!

It is such fun to be able to present these works with their original text and cover art, which we hope both current readers and collectors of popular fiction will find entertaining.

Thank you for helping us to achieve and celebrate this milestone!

Warmly,

Donna Hayes,
Publisher and CEO

The Harlequin Story

To millions of readers around the world, Harlequin and romance fiction are synonymous. With a publishing record of 120 titles a month in 29 languages in 107 international markets on 6 continents, there is no question of Harlequin's success.

But like all good stories, Harlequin's has had some twists and turns.

In 1949, Harlequin was founded in Winnipeg, Canada. In the beginning, the company published a wide range of books—including the likes of Agatha Christie, Sir Arthur Conan Doyle, James Hadley Chase and Somerset Maugham—all for the low price of twenty-five cents.

By the mid 1950s, Richard Bonnycastle was in complete control of the company, and at the urging of his wife—and chief editor—began publishing the romances of British firm Mills & Boon. The books sold so well that Harlequin eventually bought Mills & Boon outright in 1971.

In 1970, Harlequin expanded its distribution into the U.S. and contracted its first American author so that it could offer the first truly American romances. By 1980, that concept became a full-fledged series called Harlequin Superromance, the first romance line to originate outside the U.K.

The 1980s saw continued growth into global markets as well as the purchase of American publisher, Silhouette Books. By 1992, Harlequin dominated the genre, and ten years later was publishing more than half of all romances released in North America.

Now in our sixtieth anniversary year, Harlequin remains true to its history of being *the* romance publisher, while constantly creating innovative ways to deliver variety in what women want to read. And as we forge ahead into other types of fiction and nonfiction, we are always mindful of the hallmark of our success over the past six decades—guaranteed entertainment!

VIRGIN
with Butterflies

TOM
POWERS

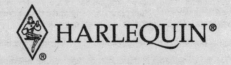

HARLEQUIN®

TORONTO • NEW YORK • LONDON
AMSTERDAM • PARIS • SYDNEY • HAMBURG
STOCKHOLM • ATHENS • TOKYO • MILAN • MADRID
PRAGUE • WARSAW • BUDAPEST • AUCKLAND

Recycling programs
for this product may
not exist in your area.

ISBN-13: 978-0-373-83748-9

VIRGIN WITH BUTTERFLIES

This is a work of fiction. Names, characters, places and incidents are
either the product of the author's imagination or are used fictitiously,
and any resemblance to actual persons, living or dead, business
establishments, events or locales is entirely coincidental.

This edition published by arrangement with Harlequin Books S.A.

® and TM are trademarks of the publisher. Trademarks indicated with
® are registered in the United States Patent and Trademark Office, the
Canadian Trade Marks Office and in other countries.

www.eHarlequin.com

Printed in U.S.A.

TOM POWERS

was born in Kentucky on July 7, 1890. He first made a name for himself in musicals on Broadway, then moved to more dramatic theater productions. In 1944 he agreed to appear in the movie *Double Indemnity*, and spent the rest of his career in front of the camera. He was also an author, writing fiction, poetry and an autobiography. He died in California in 1955.

CHAPTER ONE

THIS WHOLE ADVENTURE started when I met the gentleman from India. I didn't know anything about India that first night he bought the cigarettes from me, and neither did Millie.

Millie's the other cigarette girl, the one that was at the café selling cigarettes before me—only they had to let her quit because she was getting ready to have a baby. But she still hung around the café nights, looking to see if the feller wouldn't maybe come back that had gotten her that way.

Anyway, she didn't know what to make of this gentleman, either. He spoke soft and was not like most of the slickers that come to the café; he was more of a gentleman, with plenty of money and a ring with a red set in it that Millie said was a bum flash, though I don't know how she could be sure it was fake.

But Moe, the waiter, used to be a jeweler on the other side of the ocean. But Hitler's police cut off his thumbs, so he couldn't be a jeweler anymore, as it seems that you've got to have thumbs to be a jeweler. Well, Moe said it was a ruby, and I guess it was. And I guess that's what was the cause of what I'm going to tell about, the cause of everything that happened to me during all those months that me and this gentleman was together, and that got me into the papers even more than when I had been in court back home all those times at my brother Willie's trials. It was knowing this gentleman that finally pretty near got me in the movies even, though not quite I'm proud to say.

But that first night he came in I didn't even notice him or his ruby. I was trying to get past the big table, the one over next to the juke box, where five smart guys were drinking some Mexican stuff that Butch had sent Snowball out for. They had money all right, and sharp-cut suits and watch chains. But their hands was hot. And they had thumbs for pinching, all right. And I didn't like the fat one with pimples at all.

Still I knew I better not get 'em sore or Butch wouldn't like it, them sending Snowball all the time for some more of that Tokeeya at five bucks a crack. But I finally made a joke like I do sometimes when I get in a tight spot with guys, and that made the other four laugh at the fat pimply one, and hit him with their fists on the shoulder, and so I had kind of won, see? I forget what I said. Things just come to me when I need help bad with smart guys, things that sound simple when you think of 'em afterwards.

Well, as I said, I was skirting around 'em when Millie, sitting there all puffed out, drinking her fourth soda, gave me the eye and jerked her head towards this gentleman. And before I knew it I looked at him with my mouth open.

He had a cup of coffee and a spoon across it. In the

spoon was a lump of sugar and it was burning. It reminded me of the sterno Ma used to put under her curling iron when I was a kid back in Mattoon—before she broke it and had to use the poker.

I didn't see the brandy glass, and even if I had of seen it I guess I didn't know, at that time, about people burning brandy like what he was doing. Honest, if the cigarette tray wasn't hung on me by the strap I would of dropped it right on the floor.

I want to tell all of this just like it happened, see? But now I've wrote it down it don't sound real—that about the rubies and him and all. It sounds like some third-run double feature. When I think of all the places him and me went to and all the people we met in Africa and Mexico and all, and how we was always headed for his home town in India, and who we met there and the clothes I wore and how I got to be called The Mystery Woman in the headlines under my pictures, it is more like them cheap sensational movies than what they are theirselves.

But I don't want to write it sensational, see? Or to make it seem like I wasn't scared, not only of the places, but of the people and animals. When you see lions and tigers sleeping on their sides in a zoo, with flies walking on 'em or maybe them flicking a fly off of 'em with their tail, you don't know what wild foreign animals are like. You don't know animals until you have met a wild lion without any cage to hold it—especially when you've got hold of the lion's tail—or until you're riding a camel that's not in any circus and it turns around and bites your toe.

And the guys—say! These toughies we've got over

here think they are the cat's meow. But, honest, when it comes to going after a girl there's things they never even read about.

Well, where was I? Oh, yes. The Indian gentleman was sitting there in Butch's Café, looking into the blue flame like a fortune teller in a street carnival. And he looks up and says, "Please," as soft as petting a sick kitten. And, "Cigarette," he says, holding the spoon steady with his right hand and reaching with his left in his vest pocket for change.

It was then I saw the set in his ring. "He's a phony." That's what Millie's look had said, but I knew right away he wasn't. "What kind?" I says and "What kind you say," he says. And I knew without him telling me that he didn't know what kinds we got in this country because of him being a foreigner, see? And I knew he hadn't never been here before and this time not long enough to have ever bought even one pack. Of course I didn't know then who he was, or that such people don't buy cigarettes or he would of learned the name of a kind to ask for. And I knew, too, that he might be dumb in our language but he wasn't dumb in whatever language he did talk. And I knew this gentleman wasn't any phony.

So, I give him a pack of Parliaments and opened it for him and stuck one out. And he took it, putting four bits on the table. He dipped the tip of the cigarette into the coffee and then put it in his mouth and leaned over and lit it in the blue flame that was beginning to sputter in the spoon. And the smoke came out of his nose, slow. And he looked up at me with big brown eyes, just exactly like a spaniel dog my aunt Helga had named Spot. He never smiled at all, just looked straight at me and pushed the change back at me when I put it on the table. He had the saddest face I ever saw. He wasn't a big gentleman, or a strong-looking one. Kind of little he was, and spindly in his black suit and a black tie. It was a kind of a tux, but not very.

He had a kind of a button in his lapel, only it wasn't like a Wilkie campaign button, but was more like a water lily. Little and kind of enamel, it was. Pretty. I know now it was a lotus flower and it sure meant something where he come from, because of the way the Five Great Men, as he called 'em, looked at it that awful day we got to the cathedral, or whatever they call it, in the jungle behind that huge stone-woman god, after we finally did get all the way to India.

He had on the other clothes and the gold slippers by that time, and the hat on his head. Oh yes, that button meant something. You could tell from the little awed eyes of four of the great men, when they came up to us and touched their foreheads with three of their fingers and bowed like Catholics to a saint, though they wasn't Catholics. I didn't know what it was all about, of course, so I just sat and watched. Then they touched the other great man, making five, and even though he was blind and deaf, he showed great respect, too, after he was led up to the big, cold stone chair we was sitting on. He felt with his little brown fingers this lotus flower and then he touched his forehead with three of his fingers and bowed even lower than the other four had bowed.

He wasn't blind from being old, for he was the

youngest of the lot, but across where his eyes had been was scars, new ones. And I remember when it come over me that this littlest great man of the five had most likely had his eyes burnt out, and my stomach went all butterflies.

I always did have a weak stomach. As my pop said, instead of crying like other kids when anything hurt my feelings or things got too scary for me, I'd never break down or squall, like Willie, but I would just spit up whatever I had eaten. But that time I didn't and a lot of times I didn't, either, when I could of, easy.

Well, there I stood in Butch's Café with the Indian gentleman looking at me as if I was the ghost of Lot's wife turned into a cellar of salt.

I guess I better tell about how I look. Pop's pop come over from the old country, Sweden I guess it was, 'cause that's where the Swedes come from and my grandpop he was a Swede. And Pop always said that's where I got my hair, and I guess it was. They all called me Cotton Top when I was a kid. When I was getting my education, I studied to be a beautician—you know, in a beauty shop.

But after all the talk about our family in the papers, I wanted to get away from Mattoon—who wouldn't? That's why I came to Chicago. But too much beauty shop, I guess, is why I would never put a hot iron to my hair. My hair is off platinum and has got a natural wave. Millie was always telling me after I come up here, away from Mattoon, that I ought to do just a little more to it so it would be *on* platinum, which is the rage. But not me, I won't even fix it except to twist it into a knot on the back of my neck, which is long and can stand it.

My nails are in good shape and they ought to be after the study and the abuse I took learning to do other people's, painting and polishing. But I never forgot Pop saying that a red-fingered girl looked like she had been "clawing a cadaver." That's what Pop said. I'll never forget the word, the way Pop said it.

I guess cadaver is a Swede word. Pop knows a lot of words nobody else ever heard of.

Well, that's why I wouldn't ever do my nails with red on 'em. I keep 'em nice, but no cadaver did I look like I had been clawing. Pop kept me from lots of things, I guess, but he never told me not to, not Pop.

Ma frowned and primped up her mouth over what she called badness. But Ma never kept anybody from doing anything, especially Willie. But I was Pop's girl and Willie was Ma's boy. So Willie didn't get saved from anything and I got saved from some things, like hair and nails and lips—that Millie was always telling me I ought to do more with those, too. But "What's the use," I told Millie. "My lips are red anyway and always was so what's the use? If a barn is red, what's the use of painting it red?" That's what I told her. I didn't say, "Look at you now, Millie, from painting your lips," but I could of.

I tell all of this because it seems that the Indian gentleman like it that way; I mean without paint and dye and nails red. Anyway, I guess he did, but I didn't know all that, not till after.

Well, let me see, how can I tell it? So much happened that night, so quick, after it got started.

There I stood in the white satin uniform. Well, it wasn't exactly a uniform, just a white satin formal, with a plain, round neckline and long sleeves. Modest, see? But tight over the bust and hips. Butch said his customers had seen enough bare skin. So his idea was to cover up but make it tight. Poor Millie, no wonder she lost her job. But the skirt flared to the floor, full, so you could walk. If it hadn't, I guess that poor Indian gentleman wouldn't be alive now—I'd of never been able to drag him across that sidewalk and into Jeff's taxi, not before the cops got there, anyhow.

Well, it seems that while he was looking at me and I was watching him light his Parliament in the blue flame, the fat pimply one of the guys drinking the Tokeeya had gotten up and followed me over. But I didn't see he was following me, and then before you could think, there he was. And I felt his hand on me under the arm. And I must of showed in my face that it gave me a scare, like I told you. That's the kind of times that my stomach does like I said.

It's hard to get away from guys like that without making Butch mad. I mean when they're drinking. Well, it must of showed in my face, for this little brown gentleman put down his cigarette and stood up. I wanted to say, "Sit down." But this pimply guy had seen him over my shoulder and then it was too late.

"What's the matter, pal?" he says to the little gentleman, who walked two steps towards us and took Pimples' fat hand in his slim hand and lifted it off of me. I didn't look around but I heard the other guys' chairs scrape back as they got up.

When the pimply guy took hold of the little man I heard Millie yell. And then the other guys were there. And I saw the little gentleman rise up off of the floor, with the pimply guy holding him up with his left hand. Holding both sides of the little gentleman's black coat he was. And I saw his right fist clinched up, fat and sleek, but big and strong, too. And I saw one of the other guys with the empty Tokeeya bottle holding it by the neck. And the little gentleman's brown eyes, not afraid at all, but just sad, like my aunt Helga's spaniel. And then Moe got to the switch and the lights blacked out, and the place went crazy.

I heard the bottle break on what sounded like a head and I was knocked around like a train had hit me, nearly choking until I got my neck out of the strap of the cigarette tray. My little apron was tore off and my arm was twisted and somebody's fist shot past my face so fast I could feel the wind of it. Then I was kneeling on broken glass and I thought I was bleeding.

And then I had him around the waist and I remember how I thought "Gee, but he's a thin, little man." And as I got up somebody stepped with a big foot right on my in-step. But I felt my hands slide up under his arms and the little lotus flower cut my wrist, but I had ahold of him and I dragged him out from where they was all sprawling and kicking and hitting. And we was out of the door and across the sidewalk to Jeff and his taxi and Jeff was swearing words he was always so careful never to say before us girls. Because Jeff was from Texas and had been a cowboy, and cowboys are very careful what they let womenfolk hear them say.

But Jeff was scared about me, I guess, though he'd never let on to me. And there I was praying to God about my butterflies and Jeff saying, "Who started the fight?" And me saying, like Pop, "Never mind who started the fight, big boy, you start the cab." And him doing it, and me feeling the cold wind on me through that one layer of satin.

CHAPTER TWO

JEFF KEPT DRIVING TOWARDS the lake, not even stopping
for the lights because we didn't want to get hauled in.
And he kept talking to me over his shoulder till we just
missed, by a mudguard, being messed up by the
Michigan Avenue traffic. "Which way now?" Jeff says,
and "Hadn't we better take him and lose him outside
some joint?" And a lot more, finishing up with that he
hoped this would teach me that Butch's was no place
for a gal like me.

We passed under a light and I looked down and
there was those two big eyes, looking up at me from
his head in my lap.

"Listen," says Jeff. "If there's going to be blood-
hounds after you we'd better get rid of the little fella
before they get to sniffin' us."

"Hush, Jeff," I says. "He's woke up." But I wasn't
more than half right, the little gentleman wasn't there
yet, not all the way.

He just kept looking up at me and his hand came
slowly up to his chest—the hand with the ring on it. I
could see the lights as we passed 'em, shining on it. It
wasn't exactly red, see? Murkylike, it was.

Well, his hand come up and began to pat around on his chest like it was looking for something—something he had thought was sure there and he just wanted to touch it to make sure.

Then I could feel the back of his shoulders tense up against my leg and he begun to feel around inside his shirt and around his neck and he sat up quick. "Listen," I says, "you're hurt," I says, "but you're all right. This is Jeff's cab," I says, "and I got money to pay for it. Besides, he's a friend of mine, so even if I didn't, he'd let me pay him later."

But he wasn't listening.

"Oh," he says, not quick or scared like you'd see a dog run over, but slow like you come home from high school late and you got to where your house had been when you had left your ma and your mop and your aunt Helga there, with her little dog to visit 'em, and now you got back from high school and it was burnt down flat to the ground.

Jeff pulled up under a light and looked back through the window.

"Is he hurt bad?" he says. "I know a doc," he says, "but he's on the South Side. He's a good egg, and if he dies, he won't let on we brought him."

Jeff talks in a way that seems kinda funny up here, but it's the way they talk in Texas.

The little man looked at him and, "Gone," he says.

Well, we didn't know then what he was talking about. It wasn't his little flower button, the lotus, for there it was, still in his buttonhole.

"Gone," he said to Jeff and then to me. "Gone."

"He's nuts," Jeff says. "Let's get rid of him."

"But, Jeff," I says, "he's lost something. Look at his face."

"Please," the gentleman said, "something, please, is gone. We must go back."

"Go back where?" I says.

"That place, café," he says. "Please go back, quick."

"Listen, son," Jeff says. "If you want to get yourself took apart first and pinched next, just go back there to that café."

"Please," says the gentleman.

"Nuts," says Jeff. He slowed down. "Listen," he says, "ask him where he wants to go and you git out, and I'll take him there."

"In this dress?" I says. "And nothing else? I won't. You just keep going and I'll try to make him understand."

"Let me," says Jeff, "I speak a little Spanish. Maybe he'll understand that." And he spoke it to him quite a lot—fast and loud—but the little gentleman couldn't seem to understand Spanish.

"Let me, Jeff," I says. "Listen, Mister," I says, as calm as Aunt Helga when Spot was at the attic window and our house was burning down, and she was trying to get him to stay there till Pop could climb up the outside and get him. So she spoke, calm, to Spot, and so Pop saved him and I often thought that was one reason Aunt Helga asked us to come and live at her house after that.

"Listen, Mister," I says, quiet, "you don't need to worry. You're all right. And if you lost something in that fight with that bunch of hoodlums, just stop feeling around your neck," I says, "and feel on the sides of your head, and thank Jeff here you got both of your ears on where the Lord put 'em on."

But he wasn't listening.

"Drake," he says, "please, Drake Hotel."

"That's swell," says Jeff and stepped on the gas so that me and the gentleman grabbed onto each other and fell back.

"Excuse it, please," he says and let go quick.

It's funny how a thing like that will tell a girl things. I can't explain, but the men I've been in taxis with—gosh. So I know a gentleman when one lets go of me like that, after a taxi has started sudden.

"We'll drop him at the Drake," Jeff says, "and turn him loose and let them take care of him."

"That's it," I says, but I wasn't going to.

Well, we turned off of Michigan and shot around the block and came up to the big glass canopy from the lake side and stopped.

The doorman opened the door and the little gentleman got out into the bright light. As he turned back and put his hand out, I saw for the first time the blood on his shirt front. Just a round spot, as big as a compact, but getting bigger.

I took his hand and he helped me out.

"Hey," Jeff said, "hey." But the little man helped me across the sidewalk where the wind from the lake made me feel like I had stepped into the big icebox Aunt Helga's husband, Uncle Ulrich, used to have in his butcher shop. He took me into it once and I jumped up and down, squealing, and Uncle Ulrich hugged me tight to get me warm, he said. And he kept saying some

German into my hair till I stuck him with a safety pin that was holding my stocking up. But I never told because Pop would have killed Uncle Ulrich and been hanged. And besides, what difference did it make? But Aunt Helga knew. She never said so but she knew all right.

Well, that's how that wind felt when it hit me. And there was Jeff saying "hey" and the doorman saying, "What's the matter, bud?" And Jeff not wanting to let on.

The gentleman took a bill out and handed it to Jeff and it was a hundred dollar bill and that was a shock, I can tell you. And he took my arm and before I knew it we were inside the door going up the steps to the lobby.

As we went in the door I got a glimpse of a big black car driving up behind Jeff's taxi, and a lot of men jumping out. I remember I thought, "Good Lord, maybe it's those toughies from the café that have followed us." But a glance over my shoulder showed it wasn't them. Taller, a lot taller, they was and all with black overcoats and black hats. Anyhow, in we went.

It seemed there was a big party of some kind going on, and I was wondering how I could get him to a doctor when the swing door we had just come through swung, like crazy, and through it came the four tall men that had gotten out of the black car. And for the first time, I saw that they had the same coloring as the Indian gentleman. And somehow I knew it was us they was after. And I thought, "This time, there'll surely be no holding the butterflies." But there was.

The people in the lobby looked at us, as you can imagine. The four tall men come up to us and surrounded us, just like those quiet gangsters in the movies do. And the little gentleman said just one word in his language and took my arm and we went into the elevator.

I looked towards the door and there was Jeff just coming in through the turn-around door. The four men followed us into the elevator. The door shut, and up we went.

When the elevator stopped we walked out and along the soft carpet of the hall to a door. He opened it and two smaller men dressed in white that had been sitting down inside the little hall got up and rolled their eyes when they saw the six of us coming in.

You never saw such a room as we went into—big! And out of it opened a hall and some other rooms. It was like an apartment. Well, we came in and the two boys in white stood outside the door and rolled their eyes.

Nobody sat down and the leader of the four began to talk, soft and fast and pretty dangerous. And then the three others just as fast and just as dangerous. But, of course, I couldn't understand 'em, me not ever being educated in any language but our own, including pig Latin.

The little gentleman never said a word till they had all said their say and stopped. Then he reached up and opened his coat and snatched open his shirt. And I saw where the blood had come from. Just below the hollow in his neck was a scratch about two inches long. It had stopped bleeding and anyway wasn't anything but a scratch and I was glad.

But would you believe it, those four big men looked and stared and their eyeballs stuck out of their sockets like they had seen their mothers killed in front of 'em. Their hands fell open at their sides and they just stared and stared at the gentleman's naked chest. It was lighter than his face, like the smooth ivory keys on Aunt Helga's piano, and full of little muscles like strong men in shows that lift weights and have a light on 'em when the curtain goes up, then they pose, back and front and sides, like that.

I watched 'em stand there gawking at him. And then all four at once, they let out their breath that they had been holding and I saw that something awful had happened. It was like as if somebody told you something had happened to God. No, that ain't it exactly, but it was like that, or if the priest was blessing the sacrament and opened the little doors and the cup wasn't there.

He told 'em what had happened, not excited at all, the little muscles tightening and letting go in his chest that was still bare. And then he showed 'em how, when he'd first come to, he had felt for something around his neck and it wasn't there. His eyes and his hands told it all as plain as if I could understand him. And it seemed like I knew that what he was telling them was gone meant more than anything anybody could lose.

It must have been that thing that had scratched his chest when it got took off of him. And then I remembered the pimply guy, the fat one, grabbing him by his coat, right there on his chest where the scratch was at.

"That was it," I thought. And so I interrupted 'em. "Listen," I said, "what is it you lost? Because if it's so valuable, that it makes these men look like they look…" I says—and they sure did look like they had just come off of a rolly coaster. "If it's something you had around your neck," I says, "why, you better let me go back and look if I can't find it," I says.

I could see from their faces they couldn't understand a word, but he did. Anyway, he said no, I couldn't go back. But I made him see that nobody had seen me go out with him.

I told him I worked there and if Moe found anything sweeping up after the cops come, I could get it away from him. Moe owed me a good turn after the FBI man trying to get me to tell him what I knew about Moe not being the cousin of those Russians he got into this country with, as if he was. I made the little gentleman see what I meant.

"Wait," he said, and he turned and spoke to one of the boys in the white suits. The boy opened a door and went out. Then the gentleman come over to me and "Cold," he said. Then the boy come back and he carried a coat, just like the one he had on himself: tight, made to button up high at the neck, and with wide, flaring skirts. Only this coat was all gold—not like a ring is gold—but gold cloth and was lined with silk, as soft as a rose, and the bluest blue you ever saw.

He took it from the boy and held it for me and somehow I knew it was his coat from his own country and I knew that the two boys were his servants. But I sure wished I knew whether the other four that was so mad at him was his friends or not.

I put it on when he held it for me, and it was like an evening coat that a rich social register debutante might wear over her formal and it was warm and, boy, did I need that.

"Money," he said, and pushed a roll of bills into my hand, and I started to the elevator.

"Wait," I said, "what is it I'm going to look for?" I said.

"A ring," he says and he showed me the one he was wearing.

"Like this," he says, "only bigger. On a chain. Gold," he says.

"All right," I says.

Then he touched my wrist where his coat sleeves were a little too short for me.

"Please. Do not you go into danger even for the ring. Better you not be hurt," he says, quiet and gentle.

"I'm all right," I says. "I'll come back here, if I find it."

"I come with you," he says, but I knew that was the worst thing he could do. So I told him he'd have to stay right there, and I made him promise.

I looked at the bills—two hundreds, some fives and some ones. So I pushed the hundreds back at him and he pushed 'em back at me. But I couldn't stand there all night playing handball with bills bigger than I ever thought I'd see, so I looked at the number on the door and started. Then I saw that the four black hats was going with me.

"No," I says, "no." But they never even looked at me. "I'm going by myself," I says, "I've got to."

"Yes," he says.

"By myself," I says to the four tall ones that made him look so little.

"Go alone," he says. "You will not see them." And so I went to the elevator, and them, too, leaving him standing there in the door with the two boys peeking out over his shoulders. And when the elevator come we got in. And when it got to the lobby floor I got out. And there was Jeff, standing inside the turn-around door, looking halfway between scared and mad and smoking a cigarette, and was I never more glad to see anybody.

CHAPTER THREE

As I WALKED THROUGH the people in the lobby, I was thinking, "I'm glad the four men in the overcoats didn't get out when I did."

"Christ," says Jeff, "let's get out of here." And we did. As the door turned around with me in it, I heard him say, "I didn't like to call the cops," but just then the door spanked me and I was out in the cold. And then out come Jeff, still talking. "Couldn't do a goddamned thing—what was I to do?"

I didn't say anything, so he kept on talking.

"Here's the cab down here. We'll have to use it. I don't know where to get a circus wagon for your troupe, or I would get one."

As we swung into Michigan he looked back and says "Jesus." And there came the black car with the chauffeur and the four men in it.

"Are you all right?" he says, and "What happened, for Chrissake?"

I could see he was more scared than anybody ever got about me, except Pop, and just pretty nearly like Pop when he had been scared about me.

Like the first time they come for Willie and took him

away. It was long after Uncle Ulrich and Aunt Helga had took us in to live with them after our house got burnt up, and me not daring to tell why I didn't want us to live there in the same house with them.

And Willie being so strange and him and Uncle Ulrich acting as if they knew something, and me hearing sounds in the house at night, like Willie maybe bringing in those girls he was always hanging around the drugstore talking to. And Aunt Helga's mouth getting tighter and tighter, and then that first time them coming to get Willie. One at the front door and one at the back door. And I went along to follow 'em down to the police place and had to sit there almost until morning before I could get 'em to let him go.

Pop was sure cussing and mad then, just like Jeff was now, trying to shake off that black car that never seemed to get stopped by a red light, till finally it did, and we finally lost 'em; or anyway we thought we lost 'em.

Now here I was, and I couldn't say a word because I knew Jeff would never understand, and anyway what could I say? I knew if I told him that I was going to try to find the ring and take it back to the Drake to the gentleman without those other four seeing me, I knew Jeff would try to stop me. He was right to be scared. I should have been pretty scared, too, because I didn't know, see, who these four were or who the gentleman was. But more than that I didn't know what they was to each other.

They had looked so sore when they had caught up with him and me, there in the lobby. And why were they following me now? I could see from their faces that they hadn't understood one word he had said all the time he was talking to me in that upstairs parlour, and he hadn't explained anything. Or were they mind readers, maybe— they sure looked like they might be.

So how could I tell Jeff what I didn't even know, and him already so worried about what I had got into. Though why he should be, us being nothing to each other except saying hi-ya as I come to work at midnight, or sometimes a cup of coffee at the Greek's after I got through work. But he was real worried, I could see, and somehow I didn't seem to mind.

"Take me back to the café, Jeff," I says.

"What for?" he says.

"I work there, dummy," I says, "and I don't want to get fired. I can tell 'em I hurt my knee and you took me to a doctor."

"Didja?" he says, looking around.

"Nothing to bother," I says, "just knelt on some broken glass," I says.

"Is that blood on your dress, where you knelt on it?" he says.

"It ain't rosebuds painted on it," I says. And then he cussed some more and wanted to take me to a doctor sure enough. But I made him stop just before we got to Butch's place. And while he was getting out of his side I got out of mine and he couldn't catch me till just at the door he caught me and held me tight, for a minute.

And suddenly I felt weak as water, because I knew, see, that Jeff wanted me not to go ahead with what I was getting into. Looking back, I wonder, suppose I had quit, right there, I would have been spared what I went through that night and how many days and nights after.

But it's sure funny what makes us do things. Pop always said I was a bullhead.

"No," I says to Jeff. But I was saying no to something in me that wanted all of a sudden to let Jeff tell me what to do about everything. But "No," I says and saying it to both of us gave me the strength to go ahead.

"What the hell will I do with this hundred dollar smacker?" Jeff says, to cover up that he had been holding me and that we both knew I had won.

"Well, keep it," I says. "Have you got a pin?" So he gave me one. And I pinned a tuck in my dress where it was torn across the knees so the blood didn't show. And it looked right nice. Like a new style it looked. And I went in and left him.

Red was sitting at the table where Millie had been sitting before, and I knew she must of just gone to the Ladies', because there sat her seventh or eighth soda, half gone, and a beer for him. He never drank, Red didn't, not a swallow, but he bought one every half hour when he would come in to sit with Millie.

I guess I didn't tell about Red. He use to be Millie's feller, steady, and then this other one with the black curly hair had come in and cut him out. But not for long he didn't, see? Just till he got her that way, and then he didn't seem to come around any more.

Red, he didn't come around, not while Curly was around. Red's got delicate feelings that way. But when Curly went off somewhere, the very next night, there was Red again, right back where he had always sat watching her sell the cigarettes, buying one beer every half hour so Butch wouldn't get sore that he was hanging around, see?

Well, then, like I told you, Millie couldn't be the cigarette girl no more, so I got the job. So then she could
sit there and let Red buy all of those sodas for her while
she waited every night to see if maybe Curly wouldn't
maybe drop in, just once. And that's how it was. And
they'd argue and argue if maybe they couldn't go on,
just like they use to; that's what Red wanted, see? But
Millie was very moral and she said she couldn't go on
like they use to go, steady, when she was carrying the
child of another. It sounded funny, but she said it was
poetry to say it that way.

And Red would say, "How the hell can you know it's
the child of another?"

"A girl knows," she said.

Well, there sat Red and there was the café, just as if
nothing had happened. Butch likes it that way. He wants
to always run a respectable family place, he says, and
whenever there's a fight, he has taught Moe to switch
off the lights. While it's dark Butch cleans up whatever's
there. So then when the cops come, the lights are on
again and everything is quiet.

There was Butch behind the bar, and there sat four
of the toughies at their table with their heads all close
together and not drunk no more. One of the toughies had
a black eye, a real shiner, and the others looked mad.
But the pimply one, he wasn't nowhere to be seen. All
this I saw, in my quick look through the door, and I saw
other things, too, all in a flash.

There sat the broom in the corner, not where it stays
in the closet, but out in the café. It was leaning up in the
corner and on the floor was a little pile of broken glass

and some damp, dirty sawdust to help sweep it, right there by the broom.

Your brains are a funny thing. I tried to remember, was it Moe or Butch that usually swept it? No, it wouldn't be Butch, he'd be busy pulling the toughies off of each other, looking for anybody that couldn't get up. Cops are funny; if nobody is lying on the floor, they look in and look around and maybe sneak a beer and stroll off.

So my brains knew that it had been Moe that had swept up the glass, and I was glad he hadn't thrown it out in the can because I sure didn't want to go out in that alley. Then, I thought, how could he sweep without thumbs? I imagined myself doing it without using my thumbs, and realized I could do it.

"Well, look who's here," Millie says, coming back from the Ladies'. She wasn't walking too good, but as she passed me she says, "For Chrissake, where'd you get the evening coat?"

"Shut up," I says, quietly. I took it off and Moe gave me the cigarette tray while I patted my hair. Then Butch saw me.

"Here's your money box," he says. "Where you been?"

"Doctor," I says, "to sew my kneecaps back on. Them Mexican bottles cuts deep." By this time the toughies quit talking in their huddle and listened.

"What happened to the small guy?" Butch says. "Did you take him to the doctor, too?"

"I never seen him," I lied. Lying to Butch was easy, but to Pop I never could. "I thought they'd killed him," I says, "and you'd throwed him in the alley, out back, like last time." I knew that would get him, and it did.

"Shut up," he says, "and sell your spuds." And then soft as he polished glass, he says, "Pimples busted one of his guys in the snoot and then took something off of him and beat it, and I guess they're electing a new pastor for their flock. Looks like trouble," he says.

So I walked past their table, saying "Cigarettes, boys?" Nobody made a grab for me, so I knew Butch was right; there was trouble brewing.

When I got to Millie and Red, Millie wanted to know more about the coat, which she had already fingered, and might have tried on if she'd never met that Curly. But now she couldn't have even gotten her hand into the sleeve.

Well, Millie said the guy with the shiner had found something on the floor after the lights came up and pocketed it. Pimples had asked what was it and the other guy had said, "None of your goddamned business— finders keepers." And the others said so, too. So Pimples knocked him right out, went over him and put it— whatever *it* was—in his pocket. So Pimples took it off of him and smacked one of the other guys, too, making his lip bleed and then Pimples says, "You punks can pay for my drinks," and waddled out.

So I knew I wouldn't have to look in the damp sawdust and the broken glass by the broom or out in the can in the alley.

"What was it he found?" I says.

"Tencents store jewelry," Millie says. "I seen it, close, for a minute. It was a ring," she says, "with a glass set in it as big as your eye—bigger," she says. "Too big it was, this set, to be mistaken for anything cost anything. Anyway, what could it be but glass, being red?" she says.

"Them punks is nuts," Red says. "They drink Mex liquor and they smoke marywanna," he says, "and they fight over glass jewelry that wouldn't fool a blind cat," he says. Red's a plumber and strictly labor union, see? Plays handball at the Y.M.C.A. twice a week and don't approve of the customers at Butch's Café but he seldom says anything because he ain't there to fight—unless Curly should come in.

So I tried to sell a pack to a girl that Butch knows that brings a man in now and then for drinks and sometimes a game of cards in the back room. And this one bought a pack of Camels and beefed because they was a quarter.

Finally I got to where Moe was wiping off a table. He showed me right away a chain out of his pocket that he had swept up with the other stuff and I had to give him five bucks for it. He tried to get more but I thought five bucks was enough to buy back what may have been the gentleman's mother's neck chain or even his grandmother's, who could tell? The links were flat oblongs with tiny foreign writing on 'em and gold.

"Don't you tell, or I'll kill you," I said to Moe and he looked as if he thought I meant it but I wouldn't kill anybody, he ought to know that.

Well, I went back to the toughie's table, and "Gosh," I says, "that stuff you was drinking is sure bad for the eyes," I says. No answer.

"Where's teacher?" I says.

"Whose teacher?" one of 'em says.

"Yours," I says. "Seems like somebody didn't raise

their hand before speaking," I says, "and had their chewing gum took away from 'em," I says.

"Chewing gum," says Black Eye, "that's about what that jewelry came with," he says. "That's a hell of a cheap trinket to go busting your gang in the puss for," he says. "He's washed up as far as I'm concerned. That's the last I take from that so-and-so."

"I know how you mean," I says. "The thing he took off of you wasn't worth nothing," I says, "but still it gets you sore to think of him having the satisfaction of feeling he made you give it up."

They didn't say a word, or hardly even looked at me.

"Wouldn't it be funny," I says, "if he was to lose it?" I says.

Still they took no interest. "I mean," I says, "if he was tricked out of it to make him look a little small, not just to himself," I says, "but in front of you four that took such pains to make look pretty small, right here, where people will likely hear about it."

That got 'em all right.

"How do you mean?" one of 'em says.

"Well," I says, "of course, I don't know where he's at now."

Then they was all anxious as anything to tell me. "He'll be at Harry Mulloy's," they says, all of 'em at once. "He's got a room there in the hotel part. He's been staying there for a week."

And I says, "Suppose somebody, I won't say who, went there and was to get to talking to him, a girl I mean, in the gambling part, I mean."

"Yes," they says, "go on."

I went right on.

"And suppose she got him to thinking that this phony ring had kind of got under her skin, see? And that maybe if he wasn't too crazy about that ring, see, that maybe she could forget about his pimples and his fat, do you see what I mean?"

Well, they saw all right, and it didn't seem to occur to them to wonder why I would do all this for them. Punk hoodlums is like that—dumb.

But Pimples wasn't no high-school bandit, not by no means he wasn't, nor was he a police blotter, neither, and I felt that old flutter of wings in the pit of my stomach when I thought of me going to Harry Mulloy's for any reason, especially this one.

"What's the conference for?" says Butch, moving down to that end of the bar to get a clean towel. "You running for election as the chief gun moll for these guys?"

"Sure," I says, "that's it." And then when he turned away, I told 'em quick and quiet what to do.

They said, yes, there was a switchboard at Mulloy's and I said to fix the phone girl and when I took the pimply face's phone off of the hook she was to give 'em the go-ahead and they was to come up quick. I thought I could handle it.

I don't know what came over me that I even thought I could try it, but I patted my stomach through Butch's satin and told the butterflies to keep still, but they didn't. For in three quarters of an hour from that minute they went to town, like a flock of eagles having the hysterics. That's when I did vomit, but by that time it didn't matter hardly at all, except manners. I remember Pop

saying to me at the Sunday school picnic back in
Mattoon, Pop aid, "Remember, it ain't never what you'd
call really good manners."

Well, I couldn't ask Butch to let me go out again. The
bar was near the door so I couldn't get by him without
him asking where I was going.

Millie was crying into her next soda and her head was
down against Red's shoulder. Moe was serving at a
table, so I took the coat and went into the Ladies' and
hid the tray and the cash box away up on top of that
square tank, up over the john. And I put on the coat and
come out and sidled along the little hall to go out the
alley door, but it was locked, so I got out the window
and there I was in the alley.

CHAPTER FOUR

BLACK AS YOUR HAT IT WAS, all the way down to the next street. So I hurried toward that and I could see there was nothing between me and it. I couldn't see a thing behind me where there wasn't no light to see it against.

After I had passed the back of the Greek's and heard dishes rattling—getting washed, but not too well washed—I came to the corner. Just as I turned, I took one more look back in that black alley and a cold chill run up me thinking how dark it was. Then I turned the corner, it seemed like I heard a car start back up in there, but I couldn't be sure.

To get to Mulloy's I had to go past Butch's, but I crossed to the other side and hoped nobody would see me go by. Of course I could have gone around the block, but anybody that knows what's around that block would sure understand why I just couldn't do that, not ever.

As I passed the Greek's—on the other side of the street—I saw Jeff in there having a cup of coffee and I was sure glad. If Jeff had known what I was getting ready to do now he would have cussed louder than Pop did the time I ran off to Champagne with a strange drummer in his Ford and had to fight him all the way there. And Pop, when he found out about it, thought what you couldn't very well blame him for thinking, and me not saying a word. How could I?

Pop didn't even know Willie was in jail up in Champagne. He thought like Ma did that Willie had gotten a job in Chicago after he had left Uncle Ulrich's butcher shop. Willie had gone up to Champagne with the money he got out of Uncle Ulrich's cash drawer, and got himself into some trouble with a girl that had advertised in the Mattoon paper for a job. Uncle Ulrich had answered the ad with a letter but Willie had opened the letter before it was mailed. After he read it he thought he could use the letter and the money as a kind of an introduction to the girl. And so that's what Willie did. And that's how he had gotten himself into jail.

So there he is, in the Champagne jail for what they call assault in the papers.

Well, it was awful. Willie called me up at the beauty parlor and so I was the only one knew he was in jail in Champagne. And I had to go see Uncle Ulrich at the shop, which I would have rather died than do at any time, especially having to ask a favor.

I had to try to get Uncle Ulrich to promise me that when it was time for the trial he'd go to Champagne and get Willie off, because Ma was beginning to show signs that scared me. So I just had to get Uncle Ulrich to promise.

I didn't need no safety pin this time, for Uncle Ulrich was so mad he never even thought of anything like that and that was a relief, because by this time we were living with them and I had to watch my step and his, too.

Well, when he said he wouldn't go and that he'd let

Willie get what was coming to him, I was pretty hopeless. So I tried my last bluff. I said I knew why Uncle Ulrich had wrote the letter. I didn't know this but I said I did. And I didn't really know why Nettie, his other cashier, had left Mattoon, either, but I said I did, and that if he didn't go up there and do something for Willie, I would tell Aunt Helga and Pop all the things I knew about—things him and Willie had been up to, both separate and together. So when the time for the trial came, he went. But I didn't trust him not to just pretend that he had tried to help and couldn't. So I just had to get to Champagne and see for myself. Well, I got to Champagne and sat right in the front row and you bet Uncle Ulrich saw me sitting there, and he didn't dare not do what he had promised me. And him being a prominent butcher from out of town with money and influence and a good lawyer, he got Willie off.

And that's why I couldn't explain to Pop why I rode with that soft-lipped drummer to Champagne. And that's why Pop cussed and swore so, just like Jeff would have done about me now if he hadn't been drinking coffee in the Greek's and not seen me as I went by on the other side of the street.

"What'll I do when I get to Mulloy's?" I thought, and "What are you doing," I thought, "going on this wild goose chase? That little gentleman is nothing to you, what if he has got eyes like Spot? That's not enough to make you go to Mulloy's where you've only ever been once and swore never to get into nothing like that again."

Mulloy's is a kind of a slumming place, see? It's a hotel and what they call swell people come there late at night to gamble, and for all sorts of stuff, I'll say. And these socialites, or whatever they are, sure spend money like pouring it down a rat hole.

I remembered that night when I first got to Chicago with a dollar sixty-five and no prospects and there, waiting for me to give me my first workout was Harry Mulloy. And if it hadn't been for a miracle I might not be here now but somewhere I don't like to even think of. For Mulloy sure made it all sound believable—how was I to know what extra work there was to being a hat-check girl at his place. But except for a miracle, which was practically the entire police force of Chicago that chose that minute to raid Mulloy's place, I would have found out and no mistake. So I spent my first night in Chicago in jail, and I'll bet no jail ever seemed sweeter or safer to any girl since the world began.

Well, I decided that night that the world was too big for me to run it and so I made up my mind that I'd do what I could to get out of the mess I was in, but I knew that whatever it was that saved me that night—whether the Hail Marys or the Lutheran prayers—I sure was taken care of then and always, I guess. And so, from then on, I didn't worry about what's in the future.

I was walking fast now to outrun a drunk that fell out of a dark doorway and took after me. Only he kept running into things so I was able to keep ahead of him. And just about then I began to feel like maybe I hadn't only hurt my knees. There hadn't seemed to be any glass in 'em when I had looked, but now I felt something up above my left knee. Then suddenly I knew what it was.

It was that wad of bills the Indian gentleman and I had been playing pitch and catch with. I had stuck it in my stocking in the taxi. So I got the bills out of my stocking and by that time I was nearly to Mulloy's and I knew what I was going to do.

A big party of North Side people drove up in their cars as I got there, some of the men dressed up in boiled shirts and the women and girls in long dresses. They was calling back and forth to one another, all a little drunk and silly. And so I just fell in with them, so it didn't look like I was coming in all alone.

"What a lark," one old gal that ought to have been in bed kept croaking. "Isn't it?" she said to me.

"I don't know yet," I says and there was Mulloy. I knew him but he didn't know me. It was crowded at the place you got the chips, and he was helping the ladies.

"Reds," the old dame says, and she fished two twenties out of her gold bag and gave 'em to Mulloy. When she got her reds she moved on and he looked at me.

"Blues," I says, and crackled a new hundred dollar bill into his palm. He bowed and I could have laughed into his face. That Mulloy, I knew him all right, his smooth blue chin and his clothes like a movie actor, so neat, so quiet and so gentle. I can hardly believe it now, how little I really knew when I first came to Chicago, and how surprised I was a man could be so really downright bad.

Now I think of it, wasn't it funny that I should see Mulloy the first night I was ever in Chicago, and now to have to come here and see him again, on the last night I was to be in Chicago for a long time, though of course I didn't know that then. How could I? It was like fate or something. Like a word I learned once that I'll never forget—the word was predestination. There was a man I met who kept telling me about it, and I'd never heard the word before nor since.

I didn't know much about religion, see? Of course I had heard a lot about it as a kid, first with Catholics and after that with Lutherans, but I didn't pay much attention. Oh, I enjoyed getting confirmed and taking my first communion, I remember having a wreath and a veil and white slippers. Willie had a white taffeta bow on his arm and a rose with asparagus pinned upside down on his coat. With the Lutherans I mostly remember the picnics. Ma was a Catholic but Pop was a Lutheran. So he had to join the Catholics to get Ma, but that was the last time he went to either church—except once. So we was both religions, I guess.

But then when I grew up I met this young man that was so serious about religion.

He was a Presbyterian minister, and I hadn't ever met any ministers so I got interested like I say. But after starting to tell me one night in a park about predestination, he kept burying his face in my neck instead of telling me more, and it seemed like his hands were predestinated to do a lot of exploring. So I quit seeing him and I never got to be a Presbyterian.

But anyway I remembered the word as I got my chips from Mulloy and went to the roulette wheel. Roulette is a game where a little ball jumps around in a round deep wheel with sides to keep it from jumping out. The wheel's a lot of numbers and things on it and it turns. But it stops turning after a while and then the man takes a little hoe and scrapes in some of your little pile of chips and then they do that all over again until it's all gone and the game is over.

Roulette is different from stories about roulette. In stories about roulette, people put their last white chip on the red and then see an old friend and turn to say hello, and when they turn back, they can't see over the pile of chips that has grown up where they put that last white chip. But roulette is more like I told you.

While I was doing it, one of Mulloy's slickers with a white bat wing and fixed up to look like society—but he had too much oil on his hair so it didn't work—came up and tried to help me in case I really was society. But I put him off of me by saying, "Please, if you want to be nice, go and help Mrs. Palmer, she's simply losing thousands." He got pretty excited.

"Which Mrs. Palmer?" he says.

"As if you didn't know," I says, and he went off to ask somebody.

Names out of that brown roto section of the Sunday papers make boys like him jump like a flea had bit 'em where it would do the most good.

Well, when I had lost about half of my chips, a real society boy eased over to me.

"Hi," he says.

And so, "Hi," I says, right back at him.

"Pretty smart," he says, "the way you got rid of that stooge of Mulloy's," he says.

I looked him over. Maybe he wasn't a brown roto, after all, but he sure was a good imitation. Tie just enough mussed, handkerchief clean and good linen, but it was just stuffed in his pocket, not measured so the four points stood in a row like those little houses Pop used to build near a factory, all exactly alike.

I used to say to Pop when I'd get away from the beauty parlor and take sandwiches and a bottle of beer for him and a bottle of Coke for me, and we'd sit on one of those little porches and eat our lunch together, "Gee, Pop, I wish we could live in one of these, don't you, instead of with Uncle Ulrich and Aunt Helga?"

"I sure do," he'd say, and we'd sit there, smelling the new wood and the fresh dirt, and Pop smoking his old corncob, and we'd be pretty happy. But I kept thinking about how we needed to get Willie away from the butcher shop, which he was going back to as soon as his trial was over in Champagne. He told Ma he had missed her so bad he just couldn't go on working up in Chicago....

But anyway, this kid's handkerchief wasn't like that row of little houses, see?

"You seem to be losing a lot of your chips," he says.

"What of it?" I says. "My father can buy me some more." And he just looked at me and laughed.

"That's a pretty coat," he says.

"Yes," I says.

"India," he says.

"Yes," I says, and he kept right on looking at me.

"You don't wear any makeup," he says.

"Neither do you," I says, and he laughed again and suddenly he looked quick at the green cloth with squares and numbers painted on it and red and black and a lot of other stuff, and he reached out and took a mess of blue chips off of the little hoe the man was pushing 'em with, and I had won.

And then I saw Pimples. He was watching me, so I made up to the society kid. He laughed a lot at what I said and he seemed to think I was a lot of fun. He kept his hands on top of the table, too, so I went on talking and playing, and Pimples went on watching.

So I says to this boy, "Keep an eye on my chips," I says, "I'll be back." I started for the Ladies' and passed by Pimples. And I saw the ring.

It was too big for him—the ring, I mean. He had to cramp his other fingers against it to keep it from falling right off.

Of course I didn't know, then, that it wasn't a ring made for a human finger at all. That's why the gentleman had had it hung on a chain around his neck, the very chain that I had paid Moe five bucks for and could feel in my pocket right that minute.

I stopped as I passed him. "I see you ain't bad hurt, Pimples," I says.

"What do you mean?" he says, quiet. He was drunk. "Where'd you get to?"

"I had to go to a doctor," I says. "I cut my knees on that bottle, but when I got back," I says, "and saw your pals, I kind of got the idea they had ditched you," I says. "And though they didn't say so, I got the idea they had messed you up some and sent you off," I says. "I'm glad you ain't no worse hurt than what you are." Then I went on to where I had started to go to.

When I came back, I skirted around a table where some people were doing something with some playing cards in a little box, and then back to the roulette and my boy friend.

He didn't know I was behind him at first and he won quite a lot of blue chips.

"You're doing pretty good," I says.

"You got to watch the spins," he says. "This is no joint to look the other way when he's paying off. Who's your fat boyfriend?" he says, without looking up.

"He's no friend of mine," I says, "just a hoodlum I know."

"I'm glad you've come down to earth," he says. "I saw you come down the street a while ago and join us at the door. You're all right, but you're funny," he says.

"Why?" I says.

"Never mind," he says, "but you ought not to leave your chips with strangers," he says, "not in this place, anyway."

"I choose my strangers," I says.

"Thanks," he says.

Just then Pimples put his fat hands on my shoulders.

"How're you doing?" he says, and looking at this kid, his little eyes got even littler.

"This is my friend Pimples," I says. "What's your name?"

"Wens," he says. Nobody said anything more until I had lost that pile of blues.

"Your money?" says Pimples, suspicious.

"His," I says.

"Have a drink," Pimples says.

"Don't mind if I do," I says. "See you later, Mr. Wens," and me and Pimples goes toward the bar.

"Hey," says Mr. Wens, "what if I should lose all this?"

"Never mind," I says over my shoulder, "your father will give you some more." And we left him.

"I never seen you around this dump before," Pimples said.

"I just started," I says and we kept walking past the people at the tables.

When we got to the bar I was scared. I told you that I don't drink beer but what I didn't tell you is that I can't drink nothing at all. I often wondered why I don't do a lot of things. Other people do 'em, but when it's me, it either makes me sick or I just wouldn't want to. Drinking, or with men, or like that. It ain't that I said on the Bible that I wouldn't, like people do. I've talked about it, whether I would or ever will, or not. All of the girls I ever worked with didn't seem to talk of much else and either said, "Oh, you're sure nuts," or "Look at this fur coat," or like that till you are sure ashamed to let on you didn't, for fear they'll think maybe you're feeling you're better than them.

Well, there was a crowd around the bar and Pimples says, "What's all this so-and-so about me being let out by them stumble bums?"

"Somebody might hear us," I says. "I guess you don't want people to know you got kicked around."

"I never," he says pretty loud, and two little pink spots come out on his greenish-white face and his little pig eyes looked like he was going to cry. "I blacked the Beaver's eye and I poked Yanci in the mouth and I took it away from 'em, didn't I? Look there, I got it, ain't I?"

"Don't talk here," I says, "it's too crowded and we can't get no service. I better go back to my friend."

"No, wait, listen for Chrissake," and I saw he wanted to talk about it. I knew he was worried about getting kicked out. They're all like kids, these boys—at least around each other, that is. Who is leader and who ain't, they'll shoot and stab over that. I've seen it, often.

"Listen," he says, "I gotta talk to you. Come on up."

I said I couldn't leave my friend, but he was determined.

So, "Listen," I says, "you're just trying to fool me. I bet that's a fine ring you swiped off of somebody. Lemme see."

"Nuts," he says, "it's just a phony, like them giant's rings they sell in the circus for a dime. I don't know nothing about no jewelry jobs. You know me, I work on alcohol, exclusive, me and my guys."

"Your guys?" I says.

"Sure," he says.

"That ain't what they say," I says.

"Listen," he says, "I'm drunk," he says. "I never rightly looked at you before, but when I get a dirty deal, like that squirt Yanci trying to take this off of me, right there in Butch's place before everybody, I get my feelings hurt. And when I get like this I gotta have somebody be nice to me, see? I got a room here, see? Come on up."

"And be nice to you?"

"Sure, I'll treat you right, what do you want?"

"What'll you gimme?"

"As much as that mush you was rouletting with. Don't stand there looking big eyed, come on up, for Chrissake."

"Come up and what?"

"And be nice to me, you dope."

He didn't know about the butterflies. I was just standing still for a minute and they turned into eagles.

"What are you stalling for? Want the dough first? No soap. I work strictly C.O.D. What's the matter, you think I ain't got the dough? Look." And he showed a roll.

"I don't want your money. I like jewelry," I says. "Will you give me the ring if I'm nice to you, like you said?"

"Listen," he says. We were going by the switchboard, and I could hear the girl saying, "I'm sorry, but Mr. Grossi can't be disturbed."

Pimples was still talking.

"This is a phony, see? And I gotta keep it to show those mugs that when I'm boss, they can't even pick up a Lincoln penny without asking my permission."

"I know," I says, "but if they was to gang up on you to take it back off of you, wouldn't it be better to be able to say, I gave it to a girl? That's why I want it. If I'm going to your girl, maybe I want to let them see I got it from the boss, like they do in the movies."

"Say!" he says. "You ain't so dumb at that," and he started into the elevator.

"Is it a bargain?" I says.

"Come on in the elevator," he says. "We'll talk upstairs."

But I just stood there and the elevator girl looked at me half asleep. Then when he stood in it and me outside she turned and grinned right in his fat face. It's funny how easy these small-time bad men can be tripped up.

"Okay," he says quick, "get in," and I did.

His room was like all the rooms in Mulloy's, I guess—bed, chairs, bureau, one window propped open by a red-edged black Bible that was pushed out of shape because the window cord had broke.

Poor Pop, he was rigging new cords on the parlor window at Aunt Helga's when they came and told him what had happened at the butcher shop. And he sure looked sick when he came into the beauty parlor, still carrying a piece of that window rope. And then him and me hurrying to the shop, thinking what this would do to Ma. Because Ma couldn't never think that Willie was really responsible. I guess she saw Willie as just a little boy. But he was over six feet and ought to have had sense enough to know, in the first place, that the doctor would never believe he had brought Darlene there for somebody else. I guess we ought to have known something was wrong with Ma, from the way she was with Willie. If we had read it all, somewhere, we would have said, "That woman's getting crazy." She sure was right about poor Willie for once, and I hope that's some comfort to her, up there on the hill. But of course nobody can tell what she's thinking, sitting there. If she's thinking at all, that is. Maybe that's what we were afraid of, Pop and me, hurrying along to the butcher shop that day, me with the buffer still in my hand and Pop carrying that old piece of frayed window rope. Just like the one that must have broken in this window, here at Mulloy's.

Pimples hadn't done more than switch on the light in the ceiling when I quit breathing. There I stood in the middle of the floor while he slammed the door. My heart stopped, and two words kept hitting against my forehead from the inside of my head, "No telephone, no telephone."

There had to be one, but there wasn't. I just stood there with my back to him—which a half-witted baby ought to have known enough not to do. But I was brought out of it with a bang, I can tell you. For I was grabbed, tight, from the back.

First I saw the ring on his left hand coming around my left side, and then I saw his right hand coming around my right shoulder. And I thought, "His sleeves is rolled up." And then I thought, "No, they couldn't be rolled up that high." And then I knew he had taken his coat off and his shirt, too—and his undershirt, if he had one—and then he was all over me and I was bent back.

He started kissing me, soft and wet, and suddenly he smelled like a sweating horse. I thought, "Here it comes. Manners or not, I'm going to be sick, right now." And I was.

He had a bathroom all right and he must have been glad to see me go in it. When the door was shut I had a minute to think. I remembered what I had meant to do. Of course I hadn't thought it all out, but it would have been a pretty good thing in the movies. Like Mata Hari, that lady that they shot in the long black cape because she couldn't stick to one flag to spy for.

"What am I going to do?" I says, and I saw there was no bolt on the door and no key, either.

You see, what I had planned was this. I thought I'd get up here, let him tell me all his troubles about the gang, and then when he got ready for me to be nice to him, I'd take the phone off of the hook. And when the boys came up I'd play them off against each other.

Oh, yes, I sure had been pretty smart to think up such a nice movie. I must have seen myself, like Ginger Rogers, trailing my white satins down the steps with the ring in my hand and laughing back over my shoulders, while the four punks held Pimples, struggling and kicking, back up there by the banisters in the upper hall.

"You certainly planned to be clever," I says to myself. "Well, sister, now's your chance."

"Hurry up," he yelled through the door, and I went to the bathroom window for a breath of air and to look out. It was as black as the alley out back of the café. I turned my back to the window and leaned against the wall.

When I heard a knock on the outside hall door, I kept quiet to listen. And I heard Pimples say, "What do you want?"

I couldn't hear what was being said out in the hall. Then after a minute the bathroom door busted open and Pimples says, "Stay in here, see? Don't open your goddamned trap or I'll close it for keeps." And he shut the door again.

I couldn't bear the thought of standing there in that bright bathroom with who knows who looking in, so I switched off the light and stood there in the dark, listening while Pimples opened the outer door.

It feels funny when you're in a little strange bathroom standing in the black dark, as if all the whole world had died, and you had died, and you was all alone.

Poor Willie, that's how he must have felt at that last minute with that black cap over his eyes, or whatever they do. I felt like him, and I felt sorry to think he had had to go through it even after all the bad things he had done. But I always knew it had been mostly Uncle Ulrich that had made Willie bad, though I didn't believe Willie when he said on the stand at Dr. Harwood's trial that it was Uncle Ulrich that got him to take the little McComber girl to Dr. Harwood. But at the end in that death house Willie surely must have thought, "This time it ain't my fault."

"But this," I says to myself in the little bathroom, "this is my fault." And I stood there with my hand on the wet marble washstand behind me. "I got myself into this and I got nobody but myself to blame." And that was when it first came over me that somebody else, besides me, was in that dark bathroom. Something sure was in there. It didn't take hold of me. It just touched my elbow and stayed there.

I didn't move or yell. And then the butterflies began to act up in my stomach again. But I didn't feel sick because I had already been that—good thing, too.

When he spoke close to my ear, cold chills went up my arm and right on up the back of my neck. It was sure just like those horror pictures.

"Keep still," he mumbled.

"Who are you?" I says.

"Yanci," he says, and then I knew why he couldn't talk plain. Yanci's was the lip Pimples had busted.

"I came in the window," he says. "When we started to fix the operator, she gives out that this is a cheap room, see, and that these cheap rooms here ain't got no phones in them, so I came up. But there was another guy that came up in the elevator with me, and he got out at this floor, too, a little bit ahead of me, and he stopped at Pimples' door. So I climbed out of the hall window onto the fire escape, see? And I listened at this window. It was open and dark, so I got in. What's cooking?" he says.

"He knocked on the hall door," I says. "He's talking to Pimples now."

"Who is he?" he says.

"How would I know?" I says. "What did he look like?"

But just then we heard Pimples' voice, mad as a hornet, yelling, "Get the hell out of here before I poke you, see?" And we both kept right still and listened. This other man, whoever he was, laughed loud and drunk sounding, and then we heard something that sounded like somebody had crashed on the floor hard. Then there was a hand on the knob of the bathroom door. Yanci, like a cat, went back into the dark corner under the window. The door opened and the light was hitting me in the eyes so bright I couldn't see right away who it was standing there, laughing like a silly drunk, saying, "Come out, Lady Teazel, come out." First I thought he said Lady Teaser, but it wasn't that, I heard it plain. And it was Mr. Wens, drunker than you would think anybody could ever get in such a little while.

So I came out and there was Pimples upside down— Mr. Wens must have pushed him into a chair that fell over backwards. So I shut the bathroom door and Mr. Wens kept laughing. I could see Pimples must have hit his head hard against the wall, because he sure looked groggy. And then I saw the ring on the floor. Wens was weaving back and forth and laughing.

"Look at him," he says. "Just a little push. I came up to give you your winnings," he says, "and he wasn't polite, so I pushed him." And he took a double handful of blue chips out of his coat pockets. "Here," he says, and he poured 'em into my hands.

"Look," he says, "you sure were lucky."

I took 'em and poured the blue chips all over Pimples.

"There!" I says, and I picked up the ring.

"Good!" says Mr. Wens. "Come on," and he opened the hall door. As we went out, I turned around.

"That'll more than pay you, Pimples," I says and I followed Mr. Wens out into the hall. He shut the door, but not before I saw Yanci come darting out of the bathroom like a ferret and start scooping up the blue chips.

Just as we got to the head of the stairs, the elevator door opened down the hall and the Beaver got out with the other two toughies close behind him, but they didn't see us because Mr. Wens grabbed my hand and pulled me down the steps faster than any drunk could possibly go.

As we got to the second floor and started down towards the lobby, we heard a loud slap on bare skin, and a girl's giggle come over a transom, "Don't stop, Mr. Grossi, don't stop."

"Quite a place," says Mr. Wens, and he wasn't drunk at all now.

CHAPTER FIVE

WE SLOWED UP AS WE GOT to where people could see us and we walked out of the door onto the dark sidewalk. As we came out, a motor made a quick speeding up sound and a big black car slid up and stopped. The door opened and Mr. Wens pushed me in.

The door slammed and the car slid away from Mulloy's as Mr. Wens and I sat on the two jump seats. I was just about to heave a sigh of relief when I looked in front of us at the backs of two big men in black coats and hats, and I saw that their necks were brown.

I glanced at the two men in the seat behind us, and they were brown men with black coats and hats, too, and so I knew what car it was we were in.

I looked at Mr. Wens and he was grinning. "Where did they come from?" I says.

"You almost ran over 'em in that dark alley out back of the café," he says.

"Who are they?" I says.

"Indians," he says.

"Do you know them?"

"We were never properly introduced," he says, "because they can't speak English, but we nod to each other in passing."

And that's how it went, he kept kidding and wouldn't tell me nothing.

"You're quite a gal," he says. "And I have to ask you something before we get to where we're going. Do you know what you have in your hand?"

"Yes," I says.

"Do you know what it's worth?"

"No," I says. Just then we were going north over a Michigan Avenue bridge.

"Well," he says, "it's worth about as much as that," and he pointed to the Wrigley Building.

"Do they know that?" I says, nodding at the quartet that was all around us.

"Yes," he says.

"Do they know I have it?"

"They hope you have it, but don't show it to 'em or they'll all four kiss you at once."

"Do you know the little gentleman that had it hung around his neck?" I says.

"Yes," he says, "he does speak English, so we were formally introduced."

"Are you working with these men?" I says.

"Yes," he says.

"And you and they," I says, "must have been trying to get it away from the little gentleman," I says.

"We was just watching him," he says.

I couldn't make him out. He still looked like some society playboy—no hat, and his tux didn't look like a rented waiter's suit or that of a movie actor with too wide shoulders and too pinched waist. "Was you with them in the alley?" I says.

"I was watching the front of Butch's place," he says, "in case you came out that way. They picked me up as they followed you around out of the alley. That's how I got to Mulloy's before you did."

I remembered reading in stories that jewelry thieves were different, better educated than the ones that deal in other stuff, more genteel; they got to be.

"I guess these men would kill me to get it away from me," I says.

"You're all right as long as you don't try to run away," he says, and he lit a cigarette. "Oh, sorry," he says, "want one?"

"No thanks," I says.

"You are a game kid," he says, "and I want you to do something you may not want to."

"What?" I says.

"How'd you like to go to Mexico?"

"I can't," I says. "What for?"

"Well, now listen—quick, before we get to where we're going. I feel flattered you'd think I had brains enough to be the mastermind of these mystery-story Indians, but I got to tell you the truth. I'm not the boss. My boss is a pretty smart guy. He's a gent by the name of Hoover," he says, "and his boss is his Uncle Sam."

Before I could say a word, the car stopped, and I was back at the Drake again.

Mr. Wens got out and reached in to help me. The four men sat still, looking like statues, and I went with him straight to the elevator.

"It's stolen," I thought, "and I've got it." Then I realized, "And he's got me. Poor Pop, after all he's been through."

I could see him that first day of Willie's trial, and every day after until it was over, sitting there, listening. Then they called Uncle Ulrich as a witness, and what a witness Uncle Ulrich turned out to be against our side. Of course Pop was grieving that his boy would do such a thing.

And now that Pop was really starting to get a little old, here I was, being taken into this big hotel by a federal man with a ring worth the Wrigley Building that he had seen me grab off of a drunk gangster. And him taking me now to the owner of it to identify it before taking me off to jail.

These were the thoughts I was thinking as we came across the lobby.

He took my arm and we stepped into the elevator, and it started up. There were morning papers in neat piles on the bench across the back of the elevator. I looked down at them, and what was looking up at me from a picture on that morning paper, but the little gentleman to whose upstairs parlor Mr. Wens was taking me.

Mr. Wens looked, too, at the paper, and then he looked at me and grinned. So he picked up the paper and gave the man a quarter and held the paper so I could read what it said over the picture.

Son of Indian Prince Visits Chicago, it said over the picture, and under it, *"Prince Halla Bandah Rookh,"* it says, *"second son of ruler of Indian principality was greeted by mayor at airport, breaking his journey to Mexico and South America by private plane before he returns to—"* and so on.

The elevator stopped and Mr. Wens took the paper and pushed my elbow and we was walking along that soft carpet toward the door.

"Listen," I says, "can I ask you something?"

"Later," he says, and he knocked on the door.

"This can't be happening," I says to myself. "I seen too many movies, I read too much in them magazines at the beauty parlor. This can't be happening. It just can't."

But it was. There were the two boys in the white head things and there was the gentleman, standing under the light, smoking a cigarette. I held out my fist and opened it and there was the ring with the little beads of sweat on it. I opened my other hand and there was the broken chain. The gentleman that I had just found was a prince fell on his knees and kissed the toe of my slipper. The other two boys put their foreheads to the carpet and their behinds up in the air, and that's all I remembered, because I went and fainted for the first time in my life.

The first thing I knew was a burp from the fumes of the liquor they must have poured down me—that was sure unladylike. I lay still but kept right on being conscious. After a while I smelled whisky and my head seemed to spin around. But I could see I was lying on a soft bed with my shoes off in the prettiest bedroom you ever saw. Soft rose-colored lights and heavy rose silk curtains pulled all the way across the windows.

The newspaper was on a chair where I could reach it. I pulled it over, and there were two pictures on the front page. One was of those old Japanese men that was in Washington to stop us from going to war with Japan. The other picture was of the little gentleman. It felt funny. The only person I'd ever seen a picture of in a paper that I knew was Willie.

Poor Willie, he sure got his picture taken those days

when we was all mixed up with reporters and lawyers. You never know what a pretty little boy will grow up to. Or a girl, either, I was thinking. Look at me, for instance. I sat up and saw myself in a big, round mirror.

My hair knot had come loose and was down all around my shoulders like always, smooth on top and curly towards the ends.

The door opened and one of the boys came in with a little tray with coffee in a teeny little doll cup. I realized when I saw the little sandwiches that I was hungry and no wonder.

The boy laid down the tray on a little table and touched his forehead with his fingers and bowed and went out.

I began to get my senses back. I knew I would have to think in a minute, but before trying that I thought I better eat the sandwiches and drink the coffee. It was black and sweet and strong enough to go out and work for a living. There was a little skinny pot with more in it and three little pieces of candy that was soft and spongy and tasted like roses smell. So I ate it all and drank it all. By that time I was wide-awake and all ready to start thinking, and about time, too.

But before I could do any more than get up and look at myself in the mirror, the door opened and somebody says, "May a chance acquaintance come to call?" And I knew it was Mr. Wens.

"Sure," I says. "How long was I out?"

"Long enough," he says. "Did you find the clothes?"

"No, I didn't," I says. "What clothes?"

"There," he says, and pointed to a sofa that had only one arm. On the sofa was a black dress, a cute little black hat, a fur coat that could have fooled a mink, gloves and a black handbag. Beside these was a little traveling bag—black, too—and under the couch were two black pumps and one of my slippers. When I looked back at him he was grinning.

"Who's dead?" I says, but I didn't feel like joking. "Whose are they?" I says.

"Yours," he says. "We'll get you some more in Mexico City," he says. "Better get dressed," he says. "I'll turn my back and watch the daylight come up over the lake."

"Will they fit?" I says.

"They ought to come near it," he says. "I took your slipper and that coat that seemed to fit you."

"How did you get them at this time of night," I says, "or morning?"

"There are shops in the hotel," he says, "and the manager at my urgent request woke up one of his guests who owns one of 'em. He seemed to enjoy choosing things for you."

"I hope he chose some underwear. I haven't got any on," I says.

"So I noticed," he says, but he never turned around.

So I started dressing, and was I surprised to find everything a near enough fit.

"Listen," he says. "I want you to go as far as Mexico with the prince, and I don't want you to ask too many questions why. You are a godsend to the Department," he says.

"What department?" I says, pulling on stockings as thin as cigarette smoke. "You must have spent all of your money for these things," I says.

"Mr. Hoover's money," he says. "And Mr. Hoover's

Department," he says. "Do you want to see my identification?"

"You're all right," I says.

"How do you know?" he says.

"I know," I says. "Go on."

"Well," he says, "I'll fix it so the prince will ask you to fly to Mexico with him and his sweets."

"Who's she?" I says, and he told me that the people that travel with a prince are called his sweets, all of 'em.

"How will you fix it?" I says.

"Never mind, I think it's a good thing for you to be out of town for awhile, anyway," he says.

"Listen, Mr. Wens," I says.

"Who?" he says.

"Wens, ain't that your name?" I says. "I remember when I says this is my friend Pimples and what's your name, that you said 'Wens.'"

He laughed kind of soft for quite awhile.

"Listen," I says, "are you arresting me or not? I gotta understand some things."

"Arresting you?" he says. "What for?" he says.

"About the ring. I thought at first that those four gangsters in the big car was after the gentleman—you know, the prince. Then you was with 'em, then I thought you was arresting me. Now I don't know. I never heard of dressing anybody up in mourning to take 'em to jail, and besides I didn't know we had jails in Mexico."

The brassiere was too loose, so I was tying a knot in it. I was right about Mr. Wens being all right. He kept right on looking at daylight.

"Baby," he says, "you're wonderful. Forget it. You've

done us all a greater service than we could ever thank you for. You see the prince just got tired of people last night after the mayor's dinner, and somehow he got away from his sweet and into Butch's place. And while we was looking the town over to find him so we could keep on watching over him till he gets across the border, he disappeared. But God was sure good to us," he says. "He found a little angel, without any underwear on, to guard the little prince and his rubies, too. You're a heroine," he says, "and I wouldn't be surprised if the English king didn't make you one of his Dames," he says.

"You can turn around now," I says, zipping the dress up at the side, and stamping my feet to see if the shoes were all right, and they were.

"Gosh," he says.

"Why should I go to Mexico?" I says.

"Well, for one thing," he says, "this paper here is reporting that the prince came to America to sell about a bushel of emeralds and diamonds and rubies. Just why he's selling 'em I can't tell you, yet. But from what I hear of your friend Pimples and his little playmates, when they read that little item they might get it through their thick skulls that maybe that wasn't a taillight you was so anxious to pay them a few blue chips for. Don't you see what I mean?"

And boy, I did.

"Just so," he says. "They'll be pretty sore," he says, "and who could blame them? Now, the prince is leaving around sunrise from the airport, in a very neat little job that he bought himself while passing through Detroit, I have told him that you are in a kind of spot with

Pimples and his little pals, and naturally the prince feels that he ought to do anything he can for you, after you risking all to get Hankah back for him."

"Who's that?" I says.

"That," he says, "is the name of the ruby in the ring."

"Do they christen their rubies?" I says. "I never heard of such a thing."

"Baby," he says, "unless I miss my guess, you're going to learn about a lot of things you've never heard about before."

"But how can I go, now I know that he's a prince?"

"Forget it," he says. "He's as nice a little guy as ever rode an elephant," he says.

"But who's going to pay my way back?"

"Listen," he says, and he came over and stood looking in my eyes, and I couldn't help thinking how much like the real thing he looked—boyish and nice and ready to grin. "You've got to understand what that ruby's worth to these boys," he was saying.

"I know, the Wrigley Building. You told me," I says.

"But more than that," he says, "it's sacred. You see it was on the finger of a very special god of theirs."

"He must have been a giant," I says. "How'd he lose his pinkie ring?"

"Well," he says, "a very unexpected earthquake came along and shook him the hell off of his throne. His stone hand, with this ring on his thumb, broke off and rolled down the hill right into the front door of this prince's old father's private palace. So this hand has become a kind of talisman. So when his youngest boy started out on this trip, the old prince took the ring off of the stone hand and tied the ring around his boy's neck and let him come to America with the family jewelry, from which he has already raised about two or three million bucks— for what purpose Mr. Hoover's nosiest little sleuths, in association with Sherlock Holmes and Scotland Yard and every department in England, including Big Ben, have been unable to find out. But I just mention in passing that whatever it is that he's over here collecting nickels for seems to be of a good deal of interest to a good many governments."

"Has he sold 'em all, the jewelry?" I asked him.

"We don't know," he says, "but one thing we do know. His old man thought this magic ring from this god would protect the young prince, and the funny thing is that by God it has. What I mean is, for getting the ring back I guess these guys feel like they owe you enough money to fill this room. So you go ahead with him and collect it," he says, "but if they don't pay up," he says, "we'll sure bring you back from wherever you want to ditch the picnic—you and your aunt Mary, too."

"My what?" I says.

"Your aunt Mary," he says, and he led me over to the sofa by the window.

"You've got an Aunt Mary, see, and you naturally couldn't go off to Mexico with a lot of strange gentlemen without a chaperone, even when they're trying to repay you for saving Hankah, the ruby, by getting you away from dangerous gangsters. So naturally your aunt Mary will accompany you."

"But who is she?" I says. "I haven't got any aunt Mary."

"You have now," he says. "She's a nice woman,

young enough to enjoy the trip, but with white hair, so she lends dignity to any gathering. And what's more she's waiting for you right now in the next room, and when you're ready, I'd like to bring her in."

"There's just one thing," I says. "My Pop," I says. "He's in Mattoon."

"Would you like me to go see him?" he says. "After you're gone, I mean."

"It would scare him to death," I says. "He's had enough surprises."

"Then why tell him at all, till you get back?"

"Because," I says, "he would have to know it. I write him a note twice a week, Wednesdays and Sundays, and tell him what I've been doing."

"Your letters are going to be more interesting," he says, "from now on."

"Listen," I says, "he's getting no younger, and I'm all he's got pretty near, except an old tool box and a pair of patched overalls and a job of carpentering one or two days a week when he feels like working. You can't just send a postal telegraph boy with a wire that you've gone off in an airplane—a thing you've never been on before—with a prince, his sweet and an aunt Mary that you haven't got, and expect him not to blow a gasket," I says. "And besides—and this is very important—I send him a little money every week, see? And maybe he couldn't spend Mexico money even if I got hold of any to send him. I'll have to go to see him and explain it."

"I'm afraid you can't," he says. "You're leaving pretty near right now."

"Listen, Mr. Wens," I says, "I can see there's more

to this trip than shooting catfish, but you don't know what my Pop's been through. I can't do it," I says, "I ain't going."

"Wait," he says. "Isn't there somebody else who could go see your Pop and explain?"

"Jeff," I says.

"A relative?"

"No, and Pop never seen him even, but Jeff could do it."

"Better than me?" he says.

"Better than anybody," I says.

"Thanks," he says, "and now where is this Jeff?"

"That's the trouble," I says.

"We'll find him," he says.

"But you can't," I says. "He's hacking, or maybe driving around on the company's gas looking for me all over Chicago. You don't seem to realize," I says, "what an impossible thing it is to find a special yellow cab that's cruising around Chicago."

"You don't seem to realize," he says, "who you are mixed up with."

And I certainly didn't.

When we got to the airport, me and Mr. Wens and Aunt Mary, there was Jeff, pale as a ghost, with motorcycle cops standing guard over him. Good old Jeff—I would have liked to have kissed him, but, of course, I didn't.

We didn't have long to talk, and did his blue eyes open when I told him what I was going to do, and did he say "No!"

Then Mr. Wens took him off at the side and showed

him some papers from his hip pocket, and Jeff came right back, and I saw everything was different.

"You've got to go," he says. "I'll be in Mattoon in the morning. Don't worry now, and when you start back just call the cab company, get my boss, Mr. Worthing, reverse the charges, tell him when you'll get in, and I'll meet you, right here on this spot."

"Kiss Pop for me," I says, and I wrote the address. "You'll love him, Jeff. What about money, Jeff?" I says. "I send Pop two dollars a week for pipe tobacco and shaving soap and things."

"Don't worry," he says, "it's all fixed."

"I'll pay you back," I says.

"It ain't me," Jeff says, and he nodded his head at Mr. Wens. "Everything is taken care of," he says, "by your boyfriend."

"He ain't, Jeff," I says. "He ain't, honest he ain't. Please don't think he is."

Mr. Wens was yelling "All aboard!" He was surrounded by a lot of people, the motorcycle cops that had brought Jeff and more of the prince's men than I'd ever seen before. The four sweets, the two boys and a lot of baggage, plus a pilot and a copilot went up the steps. Aunt Mary held out her hand in a clean white glove to Mr. Wens.

"Thank you so much," she says, "for arranging everything for my niece and me. You were very kind."

"Don't mention it," he says. "Goodbye."

"Goodbye, Mr. Swift," she says, and climbed up the steps to the plane.

"Goodbye," I says, too, "Mr.—"

"Swift," he says, "Wens is my pet name," and he was

grinning. I turned back at the door and looked down the little flight of steps that was on rollers, and there stood Jeff, looking a little scared and sad.

"What's he so troubled about?" I says to myself, and then something sort of melted in my throat. "It's me. Jeff is scared something will happen to me." So, "Jeff," I yelled, "come here." He ran up the steps so they rolled a little out from under us.

"What do you want?" Jeff says, and his blue eyes was begging me to please want something.

"Just, goodbye," I says. He kissed me, firm and hard on my mouth, till it hurt, and then he let me go and was gone.

Somehow I was sitting down and something was roaring and then Jeff and the buildings moved away faster and faster and we bumped once, and then the whole world settled down below us, like it was floating out from under us, and I knew we were gone.

"Goodbye, Jeff," I says, waving my new handkerchief at a cloud and then wiping my eyes with it. Aunt Mary patted my hand and leaned over to the prince and spoke softly.

"Her brother," she said, with her sweet quiet smile, and everybody looked sympathetic.

Aunt Mary sat by me but after a while, she went up and sat in another seat and started to write a letter or something. And there I was, going up through the morning.

CHAPTER SIX

I HAD ALWAYS WONDERED what it would be like to go flying and here I was doing it and there was nothing to it. You just sit in a train that goes fast for a minute like any other train, and then it slows up and instead of the things going past the window they go by slow, away off down there, and you can see a lot more.

Flying is just a train that's no trouble and if you do hit the ground it's no worse than hitting another train, which trains are always doing. So I just looked back at the sunrise over my shoulder and decided to enjoy it, like Pop said to try to do, no matter where you find yourself or with who.

Then the prince gentleman was sitting beside me, and I says, "Good morning."

"Good morning," he says, in his soft voice.

"Listen," I says, "can you understand me all right?"

"Yes," he says.

"Well," I says, "you see, I'm American and I don't know your ways because I never met any princes before and my Pop always said, if you don't know how to do, ask polite, and anybody that is anybody will answer, just as polite, and then you'll know, my Pop says."

"Yes," he says, "he is right."

"First," I says, "what do I call you—your majesty, or what?"

"What you call me before," he says.

"Well, I didn't have to call you nothing before, because before you was just somebody in trouble, see, and I was trying to help you."

"You did help me," he says. "We are friends, yes?"

"Sure," I says, "I am, anyway."

"Me, too," he says. "Treat me as before. I like it very much."

"Well, that's fine," I says. "But first I got to give you some money," I says. "I had to spend five dollars for the chain to a man that got his thumbs cut off."

"No!" he says, and he opened his big eyes at me.

"Not last night. He had 'em cut off of him quite awhile ago. And a hundred dollar bill I had to spend to buy chips to get in a place where the ring was at, so I did. And I won some, and you are only out that hundred, because I didn't want to take the ring off of him without giving him something. Here's the rest." And I gave him what was left.

He held it in his two hands, and two big tears came into his eyes.

"Haven't you got no handkerchief?" I says, and then I saw it sticking out of his sleeve. So I took it, his hands being busy holding the money and I wiped his eyes, just like I used to do for Willie's when he was small.

"Don't cry," I says. He started to give the money back to me and I give it to him and he give it to me.

"We did that already," I says, "remember?" and we was both laughing.

"You know why you go with me?" he asked.

"Do you?" I asked right back.

"Of course," he says. "It is because of danger for you."

There didn't seem to be much to say to that, so we just sat there, quiet, and he put the money in his pocket.

"Your aunt Mary is kind," he says finally.

"Yes, she is," I says, and I sure hoped he wouldn't ask too many questions.

Mr. Wens, or Mr. Swift, as he is, I guess, had been over a lot of stuff with me and I hoped I had it all straight. But it seemed that was all the prince wanted to say. And that's the way he always was.

Pop was like that. If, some Saturday, he wanted you not to go over to Maxine Bell's to make fudge, and instead he asked you to go to the bank, to pay the interest on a loan before twelve, he'd just ask it.

Pop wouldn't say, "Are you doing anything this morning?" when he knew you were. He'd just say, right out, "I want you to do something this morning that will spoil your fudge making," and he'd tell you. And you'd feel complimented that you were a podner with him, and it brought you closer together, without saying anything, see?

Well, somehow, I felt the same way now, especially when the prince gentleman says, "Your Aunt Mary says she thinks you ought to stay away for some time, that your brother will explain to your father."

I thought for a minute he meant Willie, but of course he meant Jeff, so I didn't say anything.

"We stay one day in Mexico City," he says, "and you must have clothes. I do not like you to wear black," he says. "White is better for you."

"Listen," I says, "I don't understand all of this."

"I know," he says. "Tomorrow Aunt Mary takes you shopping. You agree?"

"Okay," I says.

"Now I send you some breakfast," he said, and he held out his hand with the little ring on it. "We are friends," he says.

"Sure," I says, and we shook. His hand was so little and so strong you couldn't believe hardly it could be both. So he left, and Aunt Mary come back so quick, I knew she was waiting for him to go.

"Well," she said, and she sat down. It was a book she had been writing in, not a letter. She hardly had time to say more than, "Well," before the two boys brought in the prettiest breakfast you ever saw. They hooked the tray on somehow, and there it was, just like a drive-in. There was flowers on the tray: fresh roses—a red one for Aunt Mary and a big white one for me.

Nothing surprised Aunt Mary.

"Sweet," she says, and she pinned hers on her black dress. The pins come with 'em. So I pinned mine on, and it smelled good, like going to church when I was little.

While we ate I looked sideways at Aunt Mary. Her hair was white, but her face was pretty and soft and kind. She was all in black, like me, and nothing seemed to be on her mind but getting sheared eggs into her mouth, with a kind of a dainty way of holding her fork. It was a heavy fork and not like any I'd ever seen.

The dishes were made out of the same stuff as the fork, silver I guess, but the cups were an ivory-colored china, so thin and light you thought the handles would break right off, but they was strong like his little hands and didn't.

"I want to talk to you," she said, when I had put back my napkin that was like a thin handkerchief with writing embroidered on it, and the boys had taken away the tray.

"Mr. Swift says you are as calm as a water lily," she says. "A water lily can be very restful."

"I never saw a real water lily," I says. "What has it got to do?"

"It's got to rest quiet on the water," she says, "just looking as beautiful as what you look." I can't say it like she said it, so calm and quiet, with pretty near a smile. Her hands were beautiful, no nail polish, but done nearly every day, you could see that.

"And no matter what waves come rolling in," she says, "nor which way the current takes the water lily, it just goes along, asking no questions."

"But what does a water lily have to do? If it don't know," I says, "maybe it won't do what it's supposed to do," I says.

"As long as it sits quietly," she says, "it'll be guided."

"By who?" I says.

"By a very wise old fish," she says, "that can't explain just now."

I got a little tired of this crossword puzzle way of talking.

"The prince gentleman is leaving Mexico tomorrow night," I says. "Do we go back to Chicago then?"

"This is a current we'll have to meet when we meet it," she says. "All I want to see you do is have as good a time as money and new places can give you."

"His money?" I says. "I won't take pay for what I've done. It's all right if Mr. Hoover wants to pay my way," I says. "He wouldn't be fool enough to put out the cash unless he thought it was worth it. But this gentleman is a foreigner, and he talked like he wanted to put out for some clothes and shopping for me. Maybe he don't know that with us a girl doesn't go around taking clothes off a man for just nothing," I says.

"Just books and flowers," she says, and she was smiling. "That Swift boy is a genius," she says. "He'll get decorated for this."

Often times she'd say things like that that I didn't always get, but she meant it nice, nothing undercutting about Aunt Mary.

Soon after that I went to sleep, and I dreamed about Pop and Ma, before she got like she is now so we had to get 'em to keep her up there on the hill.

Something jolted and I woke up to find Aunt Mary had buckled my safety belt around my stomach, which is what you have to do when you land. We got out of the plane someplace pretty flat, and Aunt Mary and I went to the Ladies' and we started to take a little walk up and down to stretch our legs.

Then a lot of men in overall suits climbed onto the plane, and the prince gentleman talked to some reporters that hadn't seen us yet because of where we had been. Then they did see us and they asked the prince who we were, but he wouldn't tell and they started toward us. So we got in the plane, and the prince paid out money in the office and then he hurried and got in, too.

But one of the reporters got a ladder and climbed up

it and flashed a camera flash at me right close through the window. The motors were going, and somebody pushed the ladder over with him on it and dragged it out of the way, and we moved off.

Everything was going past us faster and faster and then a big town was sinking below us and we was flying along again.

We settled down and I felt at home and pretty soon lunch came—it was prettier than breakfast and more of it.

After the trays went away, balanced by the two boys, the prince's men all talked to each other and me and the prince gentleman sat together again, and it seemed like we had gotten to be friends. We laughed a good deal, and I kept making pretty smart cracks to see his pretty white teeth and so we had a real good time.

"Is this your plane?" I says to him, as we was looking at the mountains down below us.

"I buy it for my brother, I take it back to him, a present," he says.

"That'll be a nice present. I guess he'll sure be surprised to get a plane," I says.

"He has some," he says, "but none so big as this American one. It is best," he says. "I ordered it before the war came, but when it was ready, after it is finished, they cannot get men to fly it to my home and no ships to send it, so I bring pilots and come to collect it. It is very nice, and nicer because of you."

Well, when we got to Mexico City it seemed like those two Japanese gentlemen that had been visiting in Washington didn't do something right, because some other Japanese that sure was no gentlemen, they came over to a place that's called Pearl Harbor and they blew it right up. And they oughtn't to of done that, so there was a war.

Aunt Mary said she was glad we got away when we did and she talked to the prince about it.

Somehow she didn't seem quite the same when she was talking to him, as she did with me.

I thought she sounded just a little dumb sometimes, and I was worrying about it a little for fear he wouldn't see how smart she was, so I decided maybe she didn't feel quite comfortable with a prince. When she was just with me I didn't know if she knew or not why she had come along. So I just went on being a water lily, and I let Aunt Mary do all the planning.

I couldn't help thinking how I'd make Millie's and Moe's eyes open when I got back and told 'em. I sat and thought how they'd both look when I walked in, and they said, "Where you been?" And I'd say, "Oh, Mexico City."

And the plane jolted and we had on our emergency belts and it landed and there we were in Mexico City.

CHAPTER SEVEN

WE WENT TO A HOTEL. It was lovely, and Aunt Mary and I had pretty rooms on each side of a bathroom that looked just like a Childs Restaurant. And we took turns and there was plenty of hot water, and we both felt fine.

It was a Sunday but that doesn't stop the Mexicans.

Our Indian friends had some meetings and there were Mexican newspapers about the war that Aunt Mary could read which I never knew anybody that could, and she could speak it, too.

We drove out through a great big park that was like having a masquerade, for the Mexican gentlemen liked to get themselves dressed up in velvet suits and big sombreros on Sunday. I thought they only wore stuff like that years ago, I mean in old-fashioned history, but I was wrong, they still do. And they take off their hats and dust their horses' flanks with 'em and bow to the cars full of ladies.

We drove away off to a place called Sochi Milko, only it's one word, and not spelled like that, and starts off with an *X* like a lot of Mexican places do.

That night we had dinner with our Indian friend and, boy, was it a dinner!

"Don't drink the wines," Aunt Mary said, "there will be a lot." And there was. I wouldn't have anyway because, like I told you, I found out very young that not only beer but anything I drink that is intoxicating is very likely to give me sour stomach. So as I say, I didn't and wouldn't have anyway but the two boys sure put on a wonderful spread.

It was held in a private room and Aunt Mary and me were both treated like we were royalty, too, just like him.

She said we wouldn't dress tonight, which don't mean what it sounds like it means, but means that we wore what we had on. It was just as well because I didn't have anything else, as Mr. Wens promised me that he would have Butch's white satin cleaned and mended and sent back to Butch by registered mail. I didn't want to be thought of as a thief while running off with a prince, which I hoped nobody would find out and mis-understand. And boy, they did, and didn't they?

The prince wore a tux, neat fitting and gentlemanly.

Well, it seemed that Aunt Mary speaks French, too, because I asked her what she was speaking and if it was Indian—which wouldn't have surprised me—but she said it was French. And the prince gentleman seemed to speak French better than he spoke American. So while they were doing quite a lot of speaking French I ate everthing that was put in front of me.

After the prince and Aunt Mary finished their speaking, him and I took our little doll coffee cups and walked right out of some long windows onto a balcony and drank it standing up by the railing.

There was an avenue down below us, full of lights

and cars and people acting like it was a carnival, and there seemed to be lots of excitement.

He said it was about the war, and that Mexico didn't think those Japanese gentlemen ought to have been in Washington while their friends were busy blowing up Pearl Harbor, but it took him so long to say it that I changed the subject.

I told him about Pop and me when I was younger, going downtown in Mattoon to see the Elk's carnival and street fair, B.P.O.E., which this reminded me of. Then I asked him if he had anybody like Pop where he lived.

Well, he used to live with his Pop, who was a pretty wonderful man, but now he didn't because he wasn't a boy anymore. But aside from that, his Pop wasn't very pleased with him just now. What the reason was he didn't say, but his Pop had given him a state to run for his own, and he had a house and he lived there.

I asked him if he had a wife. He didn't but his brother had two. His brother had a state where he lived, too.

He loved his brother, I could see that, and he was sad because his Pop wasn't very pleased with him and his brother.

He talked a lot about England, too, and I couldn't see why he spoke as if it was part of his country. None of the Englishmen I ever saw on the screen looked like him.

He looked so worried, like I said. And he said some things about his brother I couldn't follow very good.

"We are together in everything, my brother and me. I am making this trip for him," he says. "What he does, I must do. What I do, he must do. It is sworn so. This jewelry, I sell it for him. I must have very much money, especially now," he says. "You do not know what the war means. How could you?" he says.

Well I saw we weren't getting anywhere that way, so I made him laugh, telling him about Pop and the time the hypnotizer came to Mattoon. He had tried to hypnotize Pop but Pop up and hypnotized the hypnotizer. The prince laughed and we started to have a nice time again.

"You like flowers?" he says.

"Yes," I says.

"I am glad," he says, "I show you my orchids."

"Where are they?" I says.

"In India," he says. "You will see them, white ones for you," and he said it as if it wasn't far, and a kind of cold chill came over me.

Mexico is one thing. "But India," I thought, "is the other side of the world." And supposing I said "No, thank you," and these men I was traveling with didn't agree with me about it.

Just then Aunt Mary says out the window, "Time to go to bed," and was I glad.

When I got to my room somebody had sneaked in and turned the big bed down and the little lamp up, and they'd laid out my silk nightgown and my crepe wrapper. It was real nice.

The bed was soft and I enjoyed lying there, hearing Mexican people screaming down in the street.

"I'll tell Pop all about it," I thought, "I'll go straight to Mattoon and tell him where I've been." Then I turned out the little light.

I had never thought, I guess, what shopping in Mexico City would be like. If I had thought about it I might have been a little afraid I'd have to dress up like that Spanish girl with the artificial rose in her teeth that hung on Aunt Helga's parlor wall. She had a lace curtain kind of a shawl hanging over a high comb and a silk shawl with fringe and roses on it.

Maybe they've got places in Chicago like the store we was in in Mexico but I'd never been in one. But then when I was buying something in Chicago for three ninety-eight, marked down from four, I didn't have Aunt Mary with me.

Honest, she spent money as absentminded as anybody you ever saw. I couldn't figure Aunt Mary out somehow. Oh, she was top-notch, like Mr. Swift—that I still thought of as Mr. Wens—but, she was different than I expected. In the movies, a poor girl goes to visit rich relations when her mother has died and she's got no place to go. She never knew she was so well connected until she read the letter her mother left marked "To be opened after my death." The rich relatives always try to teach the girl to be a lady. But she gets embarrassed because she's not like them, and she shakes hands with the butler, which rich people don't do. When her father comes to visit they make fun of him, and she says, "He's good enough for me." Then she goes right back and marries her boyfriend. And then she has a baby and the old grandfather gets soft, and they all put their heads together, close to the camera, with the baby in the middle.

But Aunt Mary wasn't like that at all. She seemed to think I was all right, and she looked away when she picked up another fork for salad, so I could watch and find out which one to use.

I made her laugh quite a lot when there was just the two of us. Of course she wasn't my real aunt, maybe that was it. And it was Mr. Hoover's money, at least I thought it was then because at the time I didn't know where it was really coming from. So I worried quite a lot over why Mr. Hoover would let her pay three hundred paysos for just a white crepe formal with silver leaves around the neck, for me.

What she bought for me was like a hat-check girl's dream. Underthings, real silk, and stockings and slippers and shoes and coats and hats, but everything white and mostly summer clothes.

"Listen, Aunt Mary," I says, "am I going to be allowed to keep all this, or are they just uniforms I got to give back when I give up this job? And if I do keep 'em," I says, "what'll I look like, back in a Chicago blizzard, with sandals with hardly a toehold and a little strap around up my ankles. I'll freeze," I says.

"You won't freeze this winter." That's all she would say, and then she went right on choosing.

"You've got good taste," she says to me in one store where I turned down a hat with too much folderol. "Where'd you learn it?"

"From Pop," I says, "he taught me. We was always pretending when I was little that we was podners," I says, "and when we took on a job we use to talk over how we'd build it. If the thing's got any shape of its own, for God's sake don't spoil that with gee-gaws and trimming, he'd say."

"Well, you've sure got a shape," she says. "It's a pleasure to buy clothes that hang so well on what you're buying 'em to hang on," and she went right on buying.

I liked one suit, the color of a green apple, but "No," she says, "I like it, too, but he likes you in white."

"But he's leaving tonight," I said.

She didn't say a word to that, but bought me a white wool sports coat with a hood that Hedy Lamarr would give her eyeteeth to get into just once.

When the man in a place we'd bought a lot in said: "Twenty-six hundred paysos," I expected her to give it all back, but Aunt Mary just opened her purse and peeled off some of that foreign money, gave him some directions and out we went.

This took all day. We had dinner in the dining room at the hotel, me still all in black and her, too.

"Are we going to say goodbye to 'em?" I says. "It's getting late, and they'll be taking off. Are we going to see 'em?"

"At the airport," she says, "if you want to."

"Of course I want to. I feel real friendly toward him. He's a nice little gentleman," I says.

"He is indeed," she says. "I keep finding myself liking him, in spite of everything. I never like to let people get to me in these cases, but he is certainly a nice youngster," she says.

"What cases?" I says. "Or is that no question for a water lily?"

"What I mean is that I really hate to have to say goodbye to him," she says.

"Me, too," I says.

"Well, we'll see," she says, with her quiet little smile.

I never had more fun with anybody than I did with Aunt Mary—except Pop—and she liked me, too. As we came out of the big dining room, where all the people seemed to be looking at us instead of eating their dinner, Aunt Mary put her hand on my wrist.

"How'd you like to have your picture taken?" she says.

Just as we got to the door and the head waiters were bowing, some men that had been sitting in chairs in the hall got up and flashed quite a lot of those bulbs at us while all the people looked. I wanted to duck, but Aunt Mary says softly, without looking at me, "Let 'em flash, what do you care? The poor boys have to to get what they're sent out to get, or their bosses won't give 'em a cigar at Christmas," she says.

So we walked slow to the elevator and they took a lot of pictures.

Upstairs our boxes of purchases had been delivered, so I opened the white broadcloth suit she bought me and the Hedy Lamarr sport coat with the hood down the back and some stockings and white shoes that was laid there handy.

"Why not try 'em on?" she says, and I couldn't help feeling like a little girl that's visiting her cousin and trying on all of her clothes.

"I look like I was advertising something," I says, "all in white like I am."

"Something pretty nice, if you ask me," Aunt Mary says, putting my black things in a bag. "Come on, it's time to go." And it was, so we did.

As we got in the car I saw the bellboy put our two little bags in the back so I knew it was goodbye to this hotel.

And when we got to the airport, there was our plane—I mean his plane. The things on the front were spinning around, ready to go. The two boys opened the car door and the prince walked up the steps, standing in the door of the plane waiting for us. We went up and all three of us sat down in the plane and talked.

While we were sitting there, there was a sort of a long swush and a bumping like, and a great big plane came down and eased up near us. Then all of a sudden, somebody came running up the front steps of our plane, and who was it but Mr. Wens. I can't seem to remember Swift, so I better just call him Wens.

Well, there he was, in a tweed suit and a bright tie and a hat turned down across the front that no matter how much a movie actor, a gangster or a politician pays for one, or how they put it on, their hats never look the least bit like Esquire and the Vanderbilts at the races— or people at poleo games—and that's how his did. He took it off to speak to the prince, and then put it on the back of his brown head and took a roll of newspapers out from under his arm and spread 'em out. And "Hi," he says to me, looking over my white clothes. "Ah, the Snow Queen," he says. And he grinned his nice grin.

So he opened the Chicago papers, and there was "War" all over 'em. Then he opened up the inside, and I opened my eyes. There we was, Aunt Mary and me, sitting in the plane, all in black, and looking like somebody that had their picture taken going to a politician's funeral. And then I saw the headline.

"Mystery Woman Flies with Indian Prince. Is Mystery Blonde to be Bride of Rookh? Ash-Blond Beauty Flies South with Prince," and that kind of thing.

Poor Pop, was I glad Jeff had said he'd go to Mattoon.

Well, the prince gentleman kept frowning and shaking his head, and looking up at me with big, worried eyes, like brown velvet buttons, and then he talked to Aunt Mary and Mr. Wens in French.

They all stopped and looked at me, and I stopped reading the papers. They didn't know anything, anyway, but were just guessing who I could be. You would have thought I was Veronica Lake the way they said I looked—not that that could make anybody conceited because when the little McComber girl was dead, all the Chicago papers said she was a beautiful girl. And she wasn't really, not like some other girls Uncle Ulrich and Willie got mixed up with.

But every paper has got to say a girl is beautiful. So I knew not to think I was a glamour girl just because the paper said I was.

Finally Mr. Wens took a deep breath and spoke to me.

"Well, babe," he says, "looks like you've kind of stumbled into the news."

"Nobody wouldn't ever recognize me from the description," I says.

"Your modesty becomes you," he says, "but unfortunately there's the pictures those Texas boys took to prove you wrong and them right," he says.

"Thank you," I says. "Do you think Mr. Pimples and his pals will believe I knew what I was trading them blues for?" I says.

"They won't miss, baby," he says, "and I thought it my simple duty as a Boy Scout to fly down here and whisper to you that even the war won't keep you from your little hour of fame, if you was to come back right now," he says.

"I can see that," I says, "and even this much fame, as you call it, don't please me none when I think of them rowdies reading about it. I sure am a little troubled, but more than that I sure hope Jeff went to Mattoon to explain to my Pop before he sees this layout."

"I just put him on the train," he says.

"Jeff don't drink," I says.

"Correction," he says. "I accompanied him to the station, procured him a ticket—roundtrip—ushered him to the gate and waved until he was out of sight around the water tank."

"That's better," I says. "There's so few taxi drivers that don't that you hadn't ought to sound like he did, when he don't."

"I apologize," he says.

"Listen," I says, "where'll I go?"

"Well," he says, "the prince is just ready to take off for a town not so far from here."

"What town?" I says.

"It's called Rio," he says, "and I gather he'd be pleased to have you and your aunt Mary tag along," he says.

"But he's going right now," I whispered, "and I'm worried what Mr. Hoover will say if we was just to run off now, even over to that other town, with only two little bags that we got in the car, and leave behind us somewhere a lot of clothes we paid a lot too much of his money for," I says.

"Well, it just happens," he says, "that your aunt Mary sent 'em all to the airport here," he says, "thinking you and she would have to start out, after the prince leaves, to look for another hotel where they won't take a picture for the papers of every spoonful you put in your pretty little mouth. But now if you agree," he says, "we would just load 'em all into this plane, press the starting button and do a style show for the folks in Rio," he says.

It all sounded too easy to me.

I looked at Aunt Mary and she was telling directions to our Mexican chauffeur that had driven us ever since we got here, and the two boys helped him open the back of the car. Out came not only our two little bags, but all the boxes of everything we had bought with Mr. Hoover's money.

I looked at Aunt Mary and she looked at me very serious, and then she winked slow at me.

So, "What can I lose?" I says, and that's how I went to Rio, which is a big city with Jesus blessing it from a mountain top.

I didn't know Mexico was so big, because it took us quite a long time to get to Rio. But I guess we took some side trips maybe, because we seemed to stop a good deal.

Well, before we started, Mr. Wens said goodbye and told the prince he better get going as some cars full of flashbulbs and reporters to go with 'em was driving up.

Just as the steps were pulled away and the copilot was shutting the door, Mr. Wens waved a letter at me from the ground, and I punched the copilot in the back. I pointed to Mr. Wens and he reached down and got the letter for me. It was from Jeff, so I don't remember leaving Mexico City, or even remember seeing the boys change the plane from a sitting room plane into a bedroom plane, because I was reading Jeff's letter and then thinking about it. And while I did go to bed and get up and do all the things like brushing my hair in the small ladies' place, which I may as well say was the gentlemen's place for the same things also, I hardly knew what I was doing till I got to Rio, and hardly then.

The letter didn't have a beginning, like we was taught to write 'em in school. It just started. I'd still have it, only it's somewhere on the bottom of the Indian ocean, I guess. But I remember every word of it and why wouldn't I, as it's the first love letter I ever got, if you can call it that.

"If you can't start more stuff," that's how it started, and it went on:

I guess there never was such a gal, since the dudes ran Calamity Jane off the ranges. All you got to do is to sell one pack of Parliaments to a foreigner, and what happens? The town turns into a mystery thriller, with you and me being chased over Chicago by Keystone comics. You dress up in a coat of many colors. You disappear from Butch's like you had sunk through a rat hole. I go crazy and drive all the gas out of the Yellow Company's bus looking for you, only to get pinched by an escort of motor cops, like I was Miss America. They ride herd on me, till they corral me at the airport and me swearing all the way that they've got the wrong murder and that whatever it is I never done it.

And we get there and, by God, if it ain't you dressed in mourning for your lost sanity. And I say, what the hell? As who wouldn't? And you say, excuse me please, I've got no time to explain, as I am just about to step into my private plane with a bunch of strangers and also with my aunt Mary who I never saw or heard of till this minute, and please, you just go to this address and explain to my poor old pop, so it won't worry him at all, that I got to go away now with these strangers to foreign parts, because a little gang of hoodlums, that I just stole the ruby eye of the Great Spinx from, is sure to plug me full of lead if I don't vamoos. And then you say that all of this has been engineered by the FBI—that you had forgotten to tell me you was a member of. That being the case, I agree to talk to your pop, not knowing at that time that you have just that morning gotten us into a war with Japan, and that you are probably flying off now to be a general in it.

And then, all of a sudden, there you stand on the top of those steps that are getting ready to pull away any minute and let that damn plane take you off into the sky, where I'll never maybe see you again. You look so young and pretty and pale and sweet, and sure needing somebody to take care of you, and how you kept that way, God only knows. My poor old bow legs went like macaroni, and it took me a year to get up them steps to you and to get my arms around you, so slim and soft, and so good. And I can't say a damn word because the tears keep choking me, till I croak like a bawling calf being branded by a tenderfoot. And oh, my darling, darling sweetheart, don't forget me. And please be careful, because I just couldn't stand it if anything was to happen to you before I get you back to me again safe. Your friend and well-wisher, Jefferson Davis Wade

P. S. After I go to tell your pop, I guess I better join the army, as I am an officer in the State Guard. Maybe I could be of some use, I hope. See you in Tokyo.
J.D.W.

CHAPTER EIGHT

TRAVELING IS JUST ALIKE, whether you are in a boxcar with Pop and Willie when you're a little girl going to Springfield, or a big girl riding to Champagne with a fly drummer you never saw before.

Traveling is waiting to get there—that is if you know where you're going. Or traveling can be getting on a train by yourself to go to Chicago, with a ticket that you've just bought and one dollar and sixty-five cents left, after making Pop take what you had, and both of you determined not to cry, because you can't stay in the house now with Uncle Ulrich. Pop can because he don't know like you do, and it's all over anyway—nothing will bring Willie back now.

Anyway, traveling is pretty much the same, even when you don't know where you're going. You just sit there until you stop, eating nice lunches and breakfasts with flowers on 'em. And not worrying about getting there, because Aunt Mary seems comfortable and the places you stop in are all foreign anyway.

In school my geography book was just too big to carry, so I used to hide it in the Girls' washroom, back of the john. Maybe that's where I got the idea for a place to hide the cigarette tray and the cash box at Butch's. I often wondered whether it would be there when I got back, and if somebody found it, whether Butch would think I'd stolen the cash box. But he wouldn't think that, not after what happened last Thanksgiving night—or rather the next night when the mother of the drunk society girl came in to ask if she couldn't maybe pay for any damage that her daughter might have done. I took her aside into the Ladies' and gave her back the big fat wad of bills her daughter had given to me just before she passed out. But Butch listened at the door so he knew I had had it since last night and hadn't said a word to anybody. And Butch said he thought I was sure nuts. But I noticed, after that, whenever there was trouble and the lights were snapped off, I'd feel Butch's roll pressed into my hand.

Traveling is fun, too, when you come to see that people that sure looked strange at first, because they maybe was a different color from other people, are just like the other people, only of a different color maybe, or of a different religion.

I learned that traveling. Like that time I was laughing with one of the boys (that I called Bill) at the other boy (that I called Coo) because Coo slipped on something slippery and fell right down on his fanny holding a big bowl of soup in both of his hands that he couldn't let go of. So Bill couldn't help laughing, which he does in a kind of a squeal. Through silly little things like that, we all seemed to get to be better friends than before.

Traveling to Rio was nice, even if I couldn't be sure whether this was where I got out and wave goodbye, or whether I go on to wherever the prince and his sweet and Bill and Coo were going to.

But Aunt Mary was with me, and Aunt Mary is somebody I just love because somehow she makes me feel safe and comfortable. And when I say I wish I knew about a lot of things that I don't know, she says they are not as important as being "pure in heart." Even though I didn't know exactly what Aunt Mary meant, it made me feel good.

Aunt Mary was always saying things like, "No, I don't believe I'd wear that suit to dinner in the Panama Hotel because it will maybe be a big party and maybe it's a good time to wear the ivory satin dinner dress." And I knew she thought they'd all be in their formals for dinner, and they were, so I was glad I wore my formals because I sure wouldn't have if Aunt Mary hadn't given me the courage to dress up quite so much.

And Aunt Mary was always somewhere else, or just starting to go somewhere or do something else if the prince wanted to sit down and talk. She nearly always had some shopping to do, mostly for me, when it was time to start out for a drive in the two-horse carriage that we had all planned to take together. So he and I went alone, and he bought white flowers for me and the whole sweet began to treat me with respect.

The prince talked quite a lot to me now about his pop and his brother, and I talked quite a lot about mine— that's how you get to be friends. He told me something about why he was flying around the world like this; it was to sell a lot of stuff that had been laying around in their cellar, under his papa's house. He had sold a lot of this stuff in America and was going to sell the biggest one of all to a kind of king in a place that he called the Soodan. Then he was going home to take the money to his brother and to settle something between them. A blood brotherhood was the best he could say it, and he showed me a little scar on his wrist. He said the little lotus button was a sign of it, too.

I laughed and said, "Well, I guess I'm pretty near a sister to the two of you," and he said "Why?" and I said, "Because when I was getting you out of Butch's place— draggin' you with my hands around you, under the arms—I scratched my wrist on that little lotus button, just where your wrist is cut. "And it bled a little, too, so I guess I kind of belong to this blood brotherhood, along with you and him." I showed him the place on my wrist.

Well, you would have thought I had told him that my grandpop was the king of India. He kissed the place to make it well, and he looked at me till I had to look somewhere else.

"Now you understand," he said. "What my brother do, I must do."

"Why?" I says. "I don't see that."

"The bond," he says, "the oath. You must not be bound as we are bound, you must be free. As I am not free. But the English will never understand these things."

"Listen," I says, "you don't have to do anything you don't think is right. If you've made a bargain with your brother, you can get out of it the same way you got in. If you made an oath or a prayer about it you just go to the same place with your brother and unmake it," I says. "Will you promise?" I says.

"I will never make another promise," he says. "I made one with my brother and that one will break my father's heart."

He didn't ever ask me not to, but somehow I felt like maybe he would rather I didn't tell anybody about things he said when we talked like this, and as Aunt Mary was all I had, I didn't, not a word.

I asked him about Rio, and he said we was going to stop there for a minute to pick up a friend. This was on our way back from wherever we'd been, as we drove slow in the sunset with the ocean on the other side from where it was on the way out. What he had told me about picking up a friend seemed like more or less a confidence, but anyway for some reason I never told Aunt Mary.

The next place we stopped Aunt Mary went with us to see some old ruins of a place as big as the Stevens Hotel, but it wasn't there anymore. It was all mostly nothing but stones that had fallen down off of each other and got run over by a lot of vines and stuff. But there was one place like a church with stone seats around the sides and Aunt Mary said she wanted to draw a picture of a kind of an idol or a statue of a very ugly woman that sure needed a brassiere, so she sat down and drew it. I didn't know she could but she could, and she didn't leave anything out.

Me and the prince went up some steps that wasn't going anywhere anymore. We sat down in the sun and he smoked a cigarette.

I didn't ask questions and only talked when he wanted to talk about things, but now he did again, so we did.

I felt sorry for him, having to go all over the world

selling stuff to get him and his brother out of trouble. I told him that I hoped he wouldn't go haywire just because they was in trouble and sell this Soodan king anything his pop wouldn't want to part with.

"What do you mean?" he said.

"I mean, I hope you ain't figuring to get rid of Hankah," I says, "because your father wouldn't think that was right, and neither would I… Listen," I says, "jumping around over the face of the earth selling second-hand jewelry is all right—and collecting the money must be fun—but suppose we was to crash down into some of these jungles, then what would happen? I mean with us and all the money dead and lost, wouldn't your brother have to take the rap for whatever it is you and him have been doing together? That ought to make you scared to collect all of this and go all over Mexico just to pick up friends."

He laughed louder than I thought he could. Then he told me there was a little old lady that lives on a funny sounding street in England, and he said she kept the money by telegraph, and when I asked him if she might not get bombed out, he laughed again and he said she was a pretty strong old lady. And he said something I couldn't understand about her being a bank, or maybe he said she had a bank.

I asked Aunt Mary where she learned to draw and she said in the map school, but I didn't know where that was at.

We talked like that a lot of times, at places we got to, him and me. But then finally we got to a place in the sky, up over a beautiful harbor that Aunt Mary said was the most beautiful harbor in the world, and there was Christ on a mountain, and we were in Rio.

By this time I was use to living with the sweet and shopping on Mr. Hoover's money—as I thought it was at the time, but when I found out whose it really was, was pretty peculiar.

So, in Rio, Aunt Mary said why didn't I buy some presents for Bill and Coo, for by this time they even called themselves that. So I did. I also got a nice fat book for myself to write down things I didn't want my mind to forget but to remember—and I was so glad I did for if I hadn't of I wouldn't of.

I thought that Rio was a Mexican city where everybody spoke like they did in Mexico City, except the tune is different. But then I learned we were in a different country—they sure seemed to pinch and pat more than they did in Mexico, but it didn't mean anything more than whistling at a girl does in Chicago. The people in Rio wear wide black hats and they are called Brazilians.

We hardly stayed in Rio at all, just long enough for Aunt Mary and me to buy some funny hats and leather things with silver nails on 'em for Bill and Coo. They sure looked funny when they put the hats on top of their white head things, which do come off, I suppose, not that I ever saw 'em off, but of course they do.

Like everywhere else we'd been, men swarmed over the plane and did things to it—but not enough, apparently, or we wouldn't have hit the water like we did when half of the engines quit being engines somewhere between Natal and Africa, but of course we didn't know it then.

Well, they had got us all ready and just as we were about to start, I was telling Aunt Mary how black-and-blue I was from all that patting and pinching, when the prince's sweet came up in a big dark blue car. He always seemed to get something like it to come to meet him wherever we got to.

Well, up they came in the big blue car—the sweet, then two motorcycle cops and then another big car with the prince and his friend, and then two more motorcycle cops with brown faces. And we watched 'em as they got out, and when I saw 'em I sure took in my breath and so did Aunt Mary. I don't know much about people that are foreigners to us, but when I saw the friend of the prince I saw he was a friend from Japan—the country we were at war with.

CHAPTER NINE

THE SWEET STOOD KIND OF at attention, two on each side. One of the boys brought in a teeny little bag that was scratched and scuffed and about to fall to pieces. The other one brought on a paper sack that sure looked tacky. In they came and we got introduced and the friend's name was Mr. Something that sounded like Mr. Bosco. But I knew it wasn't Mr. Bosco because Mr. Bosco was the name of a man at the Elk's carnival and street fair in Mattoon that ate snakes and everybody said was wild.

Only he wasn't very wild, I guess, because the next day he came into Uncle Ulrich's butcher shop and bought a porterhouse steak. He wasn't a wild man at all; just a nice man that was only wild when he was in the Elk's carnival. But this friend of the prince's wasn't the same man and his name wasn't the same name, but it sounded like Mr. Bosco, so that's what I'll have to call him.

Well, it certainly gave me something to think about. I hadn't been where anybody talked much English lately but I had seen those Chicago newspaper articles about those two Japanese that hadn't gone home soon enough, and now we were at war with their country. And so I had to think about how I ought to feel, sitting in a plane with a little old man that maybe Jeff was getting ready to be a soldier to shoot because he was our enemy. I couldn't seem to see what I ought to do, and so I didn't do anything. After all, it was the prince's plane, and the prince didn't even pretend to be an American. I'd never heard of his country being at any war with Japan.

And the more I saw of Mr. Bosco the more I didn't want anybody to kill him, because he was the nicest little man you could imagine, smiling all the time when he wasn't laughing out loud. And he spoke American a lot better than a lot of people who live right in it.

Mr. Bosco was a friend, but a poor friend, anybody could see that. His little black suit was shiny at the elbows and across the shoulders and on the behind, and had a little line of fringe on the back of the bottoms of his pant legs. And his hat was so old it had two greasy spots under the brim where it sat on his ears.

He took off his hat when we was all introduced, and he took off his hat every time he started to talk to you, but he always put it right back on again.

Some people can say a thing and it's too intimate, and you so want to tell 'em they better mind their own business. But Mr. Bosco, he could ask you anything and it seemed like you couldn't feel that way.

The first time I felt this way was when we were on our way to Natal. Aunt Mary had said we might as well go that far with the prince because it was on the way back to Chicago, which I didn't know quite what that meant. Well, when we was on our way and dinner was over, there was Mr. Bosco taking his little hat off and smiling and sitting down next to me.

And he said: "You are going to be princess, yes?" he says.

"What give you that idea, Mr. Bosco?" I says.

"You gave me the idea," says Mr. Bosco, and he laughed like a little bell ringing.

"How did I?" I says.

"You are pretty," he says. "You don't wear paint on your lips, you travel with Prince Halla Bandah and you got a pretty old lady to go along, too, so nobody thinks you are going to be princess, so nobody thinks nothing at all," he said.

"She's my aunt," I says, and by this time it didn't seem like a lie. "The prince, he's just a friend," I says, "and he gave us a lift."

"How far are you going with the prince?" he says.

But how could I tell him when I didn't know myself? So I says, "How far you going, Mr. Bosco?"

"All the way," he says. "I have business."

"Where?" I says.

"All the way," he says again. "Business here with the Brazilians," he says, "in India, with prince's brother and the prince, too. Much business, very important. You don't know the prince's brother?"

"No," I says, "I don't know any of the family except just this one prince," I says.

"You wait till you see the old prince," he says. "He is a very good man."

"You mean this gentleman's father?" I says.

"Yes," he says. "The old prince, he'll be very glad see you."

"Why?" I says.

"You see," he says, and he laughed and took a little green bug out of his pocket and held it out in the flat of his hand. It was made out of some kind of little green stone and carved like a cockroach, only without those little pinchers in the front. It had a little link on it that looked like gold to hang it on a chain if you had one.

"What's that?" I says.

"Present," he says, "for you. Keep it always," he says. "It will bring good luck."

"Thanks," I says.

I wanted to know what had made him say all of those things like that. Only I didn't want to hurt the feelings of such a nice little smiling poor man, even if he was from a country that we're the enemy of.

"Where do you live at when you're home?" I says.

"Japan," he says, and something that sounded like "Nagasacki."

I knew he would tell the truth so I went on. "I understand," I says, "from the prince, that his pop wasn't very pleased with him, and so he gave him a kind of a state and sent him off to live on it by himself," I says.

"That true," he says, "but the old prince will be very glad see you."

"What is a state, Mr. Bosco?" I says.

"It is like a small country. It has land, many people and the prince has his own army, like a small country. The prince is like a king there, he kills anybody that doesn't do what he tell 'em," he says. "His brother has the same. The old prince will be glad to see you."

"I don't get it," I says.

"Prince Halla Bandah's father," he says, "sent his younger son away like the older son because the two boys got into a scheme with their neighbors to do what the English will not like. The boys work together. They are blood brothers. They made an oath to each other," he says. "The neighbors do not like the English," he says, "the neighbors do not like the old prince much, either."

"How far is Japan from their country?" I says.

"Not so far," he says.

I couldn't think of much to say to that so he got up.

"You keep my little present," he says, and then very soft, "Maybe also papa sent his young son away because his young son has no wife. You keep present. It bring you much luck, and you have many children and grandchildren, too." And he took off his little black hat and put it right back on again. Then he laughed louder than ever, and "Merry Christmas," he says, and he went back to where he was sitting, laughing. I sure wished he had stayed there, because I had forgotten all about it being Christmas and I didn't like to be reminded.

The little green bug felt cold in my hand. I didn't like to interrupt Aunt Mary when she was writing in her little book. It was a funny kind of a book, because in a book the pages stay in it after you've wrote on 'em, like my compostion book at school. But this book of Aunt Mary's, it had pages in it, too, but when you pinched the back of it the pages would come right out without ever tearing and could be folded once, just to fit in some envelopes she had in a pocket on the back of the book. She sent one home from wherever we were at, like Panama, where a young American man came for it to a hotel we had lunch at, and he had coffee with us.

And when we were in Rio we stopped at a place with a big American flag, and she gave that envelope to somebody while I was getting a drink of water, but I saw her do it and I came back and neither one of us mentioned it but we just sat there and had a cup of tea.

So after Mr. Bosco left me, I waited till Aunt Mary got through writing and came and sat with me. So I told her about Mr. Bosco, but not all, and I showed her the bug.

"That is a great compliment," she says. "Americans or Englishmen that I have known, when they want to compliment you, they says they want you to come and sleep with them," she says. "A Brazilian pinches you as you go by, but in my experience an Asian," she says, "he wishes you many grandchildren. And often, if you don't look out, he'll give 'em to you." And she said the bug was good luck just like he said. "It's a scarab," she says.

Then I told her I didn't want the prince to make any mistakes about my intentions. I said I didn't mind visiting him up here in the air while I was waiting till I could go back to Chicago and get my job back, if I could get it back. I said I was glad of the trip as travel sure gives you an education, but I wouldn't for the world have the prince get any idea I was expecting anything like that.

So she said I wasn't to worry, and I said all right I wouldn't, anyway, as far as Natal, where we was nearly getting to, and where I supposed we would be saying goodbye to 'em all.

"Listen, child," says Aunt Mary, "first think what this is. It's something you can talk to your grandchildren about," she says. "Why not take the whole trip and enjoy it?"

"But Aunt Mary," I says, "if I decide I don't want my grandchildren to be Indians, and that's what I expect to decide, how will I ever get back from India? Suppose Mr. Hoover goes broke?"

"There's always the king," she says.

"What king?"

"George."

"I never heard of him," I says. "Is the king of India named an ordinary name that every waiter in the world has been called by?"

"He's Emperor of India," she says.

"And named George?"

"Certainly. He's also the king of England, Ireland, Scotland and Wales."

"Oh, I didn't know he had anything to do with our friends here," I says.

"He has a lot to do with them," she says, "and but for him, my dear, I wouldn't be here, or you, either."

"King George?" I says.

"The same," she says.

"I don't get it," I says.

"You will," she says. "What are you worrying about?"

"Just this," I says, "it's one thing to thumb a ride halfway around the world, if you need it. But it wouldn't be polite to do that, and then if the prince makes you an honorable proposition—like everybody seems to be hinting that he might do—to say no, thanks, bud. Manners is manners," I says. "It's one thing to walk home from Humboldt Park, but quite another thing to start back from India, with nothing to your credit but that you've tried to live right," I says.

Aunt Mary's laugh made everything seem all right. "Will you trust me?" she says.

"Sure," I says, "but don't you come to me some dark night over there and say, listen, honey, he's a nice boy, and his folks are right well-to-do, and hadn't you better just go ahead and be a princess? Because if you don't his bad brother has got a snake farm and he's going to put you in it to think it over. I seen it in a movie and I couldn't sleep for a week."

"Don't you worry," she said, so I didn't.

We didn't see much of Natal. We went in and we got the gas and oil checked, and we turned to the right and went right out of Natal again. Bing, right out over the water.

It was the biggest thing I ever saw, and I've lived on Lake Michigan for years.

Before we got to Natal, the prince talked to Aunt Mary for awhile, and then he leaned over to me and "Thank you," he says.

And "Thank you," I says. After all it was his gas and oil and his boys waiting on me and his flowers on the trays and his airplane seat I was getting used to sitting in.

But then I thought, "And it's his friend that's Japanese, and that sits talking to him all the time so serious. Maybe Aunt Mary don't think much about the fact that we're at war with Japan," I thought, "but then she hasn't got a letter in her bag from a long lean Texas cowpuncher that's quit driving a yellow taxi to go and fight those fellers—one of whom could be a friend of the man whose airplane I'm getting this free ride in."

But Aunt Mary didn't seem to pay any attention to Mr. Bosco, and I didn't like to bring up the subject of his Japaneseness, so I didn't. And that's what was in my mind as we left Natal.

It was night, the lights were on and the black curtains were pulled over the windows. We were to Hell-and-gone out over the water when the copilot came back with a paper in his hand. He said we couldn't go to Dakar, which it seems we had meant to do, because of something about some German people and some French people, and so we was going to Libeeria. And I certainly didn't care, because neither one of those countries—Dakar or Libeeria—had I ever heard of till that minute, and so while they were talking about it in all the languages I couldn't understand, I went to sleep.

Something woke me up as if a gun had gone off. But it wasn't a noise, it was the lack of noise that did it. One of the engines quit and the lights got dim, and then it seemed like our plane was going over a rough road because I was shaken nearly out of my seat and people looked scared. The prince brought me a lifesaver—not the kind you eat, with a hole in it so your wife won't know you've stopped at a bar on the way home, but another kind, with a hole in it, too, that you put your head in, instead of your tongue. It was like a bustle of my grandma's that Aunt Helga let me put on once to be Martha Washington at school, but my wig fell off and everybody laughed.

Well, this bustle was like that, only it wasn't for the same place where a real bustle is made to go. No, this bustle sits right up on your chest, and another bustle sits right up on your shoulders in back. And the prince made big eyes, and he said we was sinking down. Not in the ocean he didn't mean, not yet, but I guess sinking down even in the air is a pretty bad thing to be doing. So no wonder his brown eyes was big.

And Aunt Mary, she was as calm as any princess that ever died for her country. She sat there by me, next to the window in her bustle. "Listen," she says, "if we hit the water," she says, "the plane will float for a little while, so we can get out of the emergency door. Now don't get scared, I've done it before," she says, "only in a big storm. This is a calm sea," she says.

"Then why can't we settle down on the sea and just go ahead like a boat?" I says. "I've seen 'em do that on the lake."

"Because this is a land plane and has only got wheels—they don't run very well even on the smoothest water," she says.

"What do we do?" I says, and I had to laugh. "It sure looks like you was right and I am going to turn into a water lily after all." So we both laughed a little.

Mr. Bosco saw us laughing and he came over to us. He smiled at me over his little bustle.

"There are a lot of ships," he said, "mostly German," and he looked as pleased as if he had said, "Nice dinner, Italian cooking." But then I thought, "What's it to him? He ain't at war with Germany. He'll go free and we'll all get shot—if we ain't drounded or crack our skulls when she hits, like Tyrone Power when his did."

Now the copilot come back and yelled something.

The prince said something to the copilot, then came to me and took both of my hands.

"When she hits," he said, "I must save you. If everybody dies you must be saved."

"Thank you," I says, "but if I get saved Aunt Mary's got to be saved, too."

"You are not afraid?" he says.

"What of?" I says, and his mouth stayed open.

"No, I mean it," I says. "Getting scared sure won't save any of us."

"You do not blame me?" he says.

"For what?" I says.

"For bringing you."

"Forget it," I says. "I was glad enough to be invited."

"My life I would give to save you from danger," he says, and he meant it. He would have, and as it turned out he nearly did later.

Now the copilot come in again and just stood there looking at us. "This is it" was written all over him.

We all buckled our belts like he had shown us and like we always did when we landed, but this time it looked like we was going to do it just like always, only without the land.

We could hear the water coming up to meet us, or maybe the sound of everything changed as we got nearer the water. Anyway you could just about tell when we were going to crash onto it by the different sound the engine made as we got nearer and nearer. We were still going forward, but sinking down at the same time. You could feel us sinking in the air and, like I said, the ocean coming up to meet us.

Suddenly there was the prince, out of his safety belt. His arms around me were strong, and he braced his feet. He was nearly in the seat with me, holding me against the jolt of however we hit.

"Get in your seat," I yelled.

Everybody was yelling now except Aunt Mary and Mr. Bosco.

"No," he says, "I must save you, I must be with you."

The copilot yelled at him, and he said, "No."

One of the four sweets said what must have been something like, "Please, prince, if you get killed we'll lose our jobs because there won't be anybody to sweet for."

But he said right back at 'em, with a tight little smile, what I guess meant, "God bless you boys, but you won't be fit to sweet for nobody when the bump and splash is over."

So we all sat tight and waited for that splash.

It took about a year, and while we sat there time just stopped.

And I let my mind run on to where it wanted to because I didn't want it to run on to what was about to happen. And then it did happen. We hit the water, and it was like when I was at the Springfield Fair riding on one of those pop-the-whips and I got jerked around a corner. Well, we was sure jerked around a corner.

It was like one wing had hit that big rock that you see pictures of that has got Prudential written across the front of it. But it sure gave us a jolt. And it put the prince right in my lap, still protecting me with all his might.

Well, what happened could only be explained by

somebody that knows about miracles, because I guess that's about what it was.

A long time after this, I asked a nice English boy I was on a raft with if he thought it'd been a miracle, and he said that of course it was, and that miracles happened so often to everybody that flew in this war that the only times they got surprised was when a miracle didn't happen. But he was pretty feverish by that time from loss of blood but still he'd sure seen a lot of miracles. To tell the truth, him and me had just been through one at that time, that's how we got on that raft.

But I'm getting ahead of myself—I was trying to tell what happened between Natal and Dakar. The wing must have hit a wave because there was this jolt that loosened your wisdom teeth. Then we turned a corner, like I said, and the plane shook and righted itself and shuddered. Our ears were nearly split a second later by a new roaring—one of the engines that had quit working was working again. It kept on doing that, and so we got to Libeeria.

Aunt Mary and me stayed in a hotel and there was a young man we met there who worked for Firestone tires. He kept looking at me—he was a college boy, I guess. Anyway he said he was a friend of the actual Firestone boys, and there seems to be quite a lot of 'em. Five, I think he said. I thought all this time that Firestone was something strong that the tires were made out of, and come to think of it, maybe I was right at that.

Well, he got me to one side and talked a lot, with his hands clasped so you could see the knuckles greenish-white pressing together, and he said he was lonesome so far from home.

He told me he wasn't the usual kind that tries something the first minute he meets a girl, and something about his pink eyelids reminded me of that Presbyterian minister that was always burying his cold nose in my neck. And then he got to talking about me and he asked who I was traveling with. I told him and then it seemed like he went kind of crazy. So I tried not to listen to all the names he called the prince and his sweet, but he wouldn't stop and kept on and on. Then I got mad.

I was sorry afterward that I had slapped him so hard, but it did get his attention and made him stop. So then I told him a few home truths.

Well, sir, instead of making him mad, or to go away like it ought to have done, it just made him feel that we was well enough acquainted for him to quit holding on to himself. I felt sorry for him and so I let him hold on to my hand and tell me all about how he was saving himself for the girl he married, but couldn't he kiss me just once. But I didn't let him and I decided to slap him again—hard enough to knock his hornrims off, but they didn't break. He came at me again, and that made me remember Pop and me sparring under a big elm tree at the Lutheran picnic, and me in my plaid taffeta and Pop saying, "Even a little quick punch in the stomach with your left will make his face come over toward you, and then you'd be surprised what a little uppercut on the point of the chin will take all the fight right out of him."

Well, like always, Pop was right.

And that's all I remember about Libeeria.

But it made me feel somehow different about the poor little prince and not the way this college boy wanted me to feel at all.

It seems that there is a real place by the name of Timbuktu. I had always thought it was just a made-up name, but it's not, because we flew right over it. Mr. Bosco was sitting with me then and he told me.

We got to talking about the prince, and Mr. Bosco said that he and his brother and his father owned just about everything where they lived except for money. He said money is not always easy for rich people to get, which I didn't know before because I always thought being rich meant you had money, but it don't.

And that's why the prince brought all of that stuff and had sold it. And he was going to sell this special piece to the Soodan king to get the rest of a lot of the money. The prince wanted to use the money for something that had to be used right quick, before the war went any further. That's why Mr. Bosco had been visiting in Rio and why we had to fly all that way out of our way to get him so he could come back and help the prince's brother do whatever it was he was about to do.

"Who was the brother about to do it with?" I says. And Mr. Bosco says, "With the Japanese."

So I asked Mr. Bosco if the brother was fond of the Japanese and he said, yes, he was, and that he didn't like the English at all. But it seemed to me that the English people were on our side, so I got more worried if the prince was collecting money for our enemies. But I didn't say anything to Aunt Mary because she had enough to do, sending pages out of her little book.

There was one place we got to where she couldn't send them, and it seemed to worry her a little. So I didn't tell her these things that Mr. Bosco told me all the time.

I guessed it was because Mr. Bosco thought I was going to marry the prince that he talked to me that way. "Well," I thought, "Mr. Bosco can't know about Pimples and why I'm here, and if he wants to think that way, let him."

But as it turned out, anybody that thought there was anything Mr. Bosco didn't know just didn't know Mr. Bosco.

So, after awhile, we got to a place that's called Khartoum, and it was just like the movies—if I'd ever saw one.

Khartoum was full of all sorts of people and swagger sticks that I never saw before, and they used the sticks to push people out of the way if they got in it.

Aunt Mary stopped in a bazaar where we was buying some riding things for me—because of camels and elephants we might have to be riding on—and she looked at me.

"Pimples is in jail," she said.

"What for?" I says.

"I don't know," she says, "but he is."

"You sound like a spiritualist medium," I says, "that's had a vision in a little glass thing."

"That's what I am," she says, "only I get my visions by code," she says, "from cables sent by a young man that's pretty sold on you."

"Jeff?" I says.

"Not Jeff," she says. "That boy that you call Carbuncles or whatever it is, and who I call Ted Swift," she says.

"What did he say?"

"Just that," she says, "'PIMPLES IN JAIL. HOPE FOR CONVICTION. PALS LATER. GIVE SNOW QUEEN INFORMATION AND MY LOVE.' That was all."

"Does that mean I can go home?" I says, while the little man that was fitting my britches was sticking pins all over me.

"It certainly means that the time is coming when you can think about it," she says, "if you want to."

"Listen, Aunt Mary," I says, "this is all a lot of fun, and I can tell my grandchildren things they sure won't believe, like you said. But if I don't hurry and get back, my job will be gone," I says, "and who knows where they might send Jeff?"

"They might send Jeff right to where you're going," she says.

"Honest?" I says. "Oh, Aunt Mary, could they, might they?"

"Yes," she says, "they might. What would you say to that?"

Well, what I said was, "Ouch," because at that second the little man stuck a pin in me, in a very bad place.

On the way back to the plane, she put her soft hand on mine and said, "Listen, child, I'm sure you know there's more to all of this than keeping you from a few curbstone bandits in a bad neighborhood back in Chicago," she says.

"How do you mean?" I says.

"You are just a decoy," she says.

But I didn't know what that was, so she said it was a duck made out of wood, that floats on the water.

"Don't I ever get on dry land?" I says. "First I'm a water lily and now I'm a wooden duck like the one I once saw Donald riding on the back of because he didn't have any mother."

So she laughed.

"Try to keep on trusting me," she said. "There's something we've got to find out in India," she says, "and when we find it out, our work will be done and then you can go home the quickest way."

"But what does a decoy do?"

"Well, it was pretty important for me to be near enough to know what a certain gentleman was up to. But there was no way to do that once he took off over that Mexican border. And then a way was found by a very bright young American boy."

So, here I was, mixed up in something I didn't mean to get into. And that I sure didn't know much about, like a lot of other things I didn't know about—like the law, which I ought to know so much about, me having been in on court trials and coroner's inquests.

That poor Dr. Harwood, wasn't he only keeping poor little Darlene McComber from having a baby that she surely wouldn't have known what to do with?

Well, anyway the law said he was a criminal. But now comes the part I couldn't understand. The first thing was that Dr. Harwood—who didn't have much money—had a lawyer that everybody said was the highest paid one you could get. He certainly was worth it, because he got Dr. Harwood off free. So then you'd think he wasn't a criminal anymore, although everybody must have known he did what they said.

But after he got free, it turned out that there was a society of all the other doctors, and they had a meeting, and they kicked Dr. Harwood out anyway, so he wouldn't have ever been able to practice anymore, even if what had happened to poor Dr. Harwood hadn't happened.

But of course we didn't know that then. So there was Willie, not tried yet, and out on bail. Because they naturally didn't believe it was Uncle Ulrich who was to blame about Darlene. So Willie was out on bail, as I said, but he wouldn't come home because the only home there was to come to was Uncle Ulrich's house where we lived.

CHAPTER TEN

WELL, HERE I WAS IN AFRICA being a kind of a Mata Hari, only dressed in white, and not knowing just what a decoy was supposed to do but going right on doing it.

Soodan is a desert, and it seems there's a good many kings of it. So we went to see one that wasn't young—but sure had young ideas—and a big bushy beard as red as fire, and robes and some stuff over his head like fine muslin, and his nails had what Aunt Mary called little black mourning bands along the edges. He was a bad old boy and crazy about me.

He called me the funniest name. He called me Palace Theater, which was the only English or American word he knew—except kiss, which he never stopped saying and trying to do.

He had a palace that was right out of Hollywood and wives with veils over the lower parts of their faces.

This king had sixteen sons, all different sizes but dressed like him. They were scared of him when he was there, but when he wasn't, oh boy.

Aunt Mary said they had to work off their youthful energy some way, so they got up a kind of a show out in the desert that we all went to, and after seeing how wild these boys really could get, I was more scared of 'em than ever.

We rode on camels right out of Barnum & Bailey—that is, the boys and me did, the rest went in the Rolls-Royce.

My camel was white and her name was Wo Baby. Everybody called her that because that's what I named her, even though I hadn't meant to.

It was like this. The king's wives didn't ride camels, and that ain't all. They didn't do anything at all but sit around and eat. They put black stuff on their eyelids that they never washed off but just put more on. And they painted the palms of their hands orange. At least I thought they was painted, but I found out it wasn't from paint but from rubbing henna leaves. And I found out where they rub 'em, too. That's why the king's beard was red like that. So that's all the wives had to do—to rub henna and get fat and have sixteen sons.

Well, me not being a wife of the king and having new white riding britches, I said I had always wanted to ride a camel, so they let me.

Well, the boys thought it was funny enough to see me in my britches, and they thought it would be fun to see me ride one, even if I got killed, which, being wild, I soon found out would seem to them like a very funny joke. So being playful, they put a couple of scorpions under the red saddle.

Well, I got on it, and the camel that was lying down got up. Naturally I sat on the saddle, and the saddle sat on these scorpions, and the scorpions didn't like it so they stung the camel. So that camel made that desert look like a Wild West rodeo for about ten minutes.

Everytime we went up in the air I yelled, "Wo Baby," but the camel paid no attention, not speaking English. So down we came, and I'd yell, "Wo Baby," as we went up again higher and twistier than the last time. And it went on like that till I had landed hard enough to kill the scorpions.

But I didn't fall off, and that seemed like such a miracle to the old king that he had his people catch the boys that did that with the scorpions and put scorpions under their saddles. Their camels jumped even crazier than mine had till they both fell off on their heads, and one broke his wrist. And that's how I named the white camel Wo Baby.

When I saw people riding the circus camel in Mattoon, they just sat on the hump straddle and got led along slowly as the camel chewed cud with long yellow teeth and a tongue hanging out the side. But riding with fourteen crazy Soodan boys was like riding behind the Twentieth Century Limited train and bumping over the ties. It was just bumps and grinds, and the camel's long yellow teeth were just the same as in the circus, but instead of chewing cud, everytime I stopped or slowed up, the camel turned around its long neck and those yellow teeth chewed on my foot.

And, added to that, the camel had a voice that I never knew a camel had, sounding like four seals at feeding time and an elephant being really sick.

Well, by remembering Pop's advice and just relaxing, riding got to be a kind of a rumba. And it got to be fun, because I went with the camel instead of meeting it coming back, and it was easy.

So we were all ready to follow the king's car to the place where the rodeo was to be at. And the boys on their camels began to yell to me what sounded like "Le's race." So I took a silver whip somebody had hung over my wrist and I took up the single bridle and I said, "Okay" and I let Wo Baby have it. And it sure was a race.

Only two boys got to the playground before me and Wo Baby. All the rest that came trailing in behind us in a cloud of our dust got a royal Soodanese razzing from the old king sitting in his car at the finish with the prince and Aunt Mary and Mr. Bosco.

When Wo Baby stopped, I threw my leg over just before she bit the toe of my new boot right off, and without waiting for her to lay down like they make 'em do I slid off the side of her.

Well, one of the older boys, seeing what I was going to do, jumped off of his camel while it was running, sending his white cape flying out behind him in the air like wings.

He landed running and got to me in time to catch me in the strongest arms I ever felt before I hit the ground. He carried me over to the car with his black whiskers that smelled like incense tickling my face where he was kissing me and he hoisted me up into the seat beside his father.

"Palace Theater," the old king yelled, roaring with laughter, and he patted me all over pretty much. All the boys yelled and fired off guns, and it sure was different.

Aunt Mary showed me a medal on the king that King George gave to him in London after the last war, when he went there to tell the King of England he was glad his side won. And Aunt Mary said that must have been where he got the name he called me. She said a lot of Soodan kings had gone there to congratulate the English king and that she remembered one of the places they was taken to in London was the Palace Theater.

While they were getting the games organized, Mr. Bosco whispered to me, "The king is very rich, he says you are nice so he will show you his machine."

"What kind of a machine?" I says.

"You will see," says Mr. Bosco, and he giggled.

The games began, and they sure made football and basketball and even hockey look like tiddleywinks.

There were beautiful horses with small heads and long white manes and tails that those boys rode all over. They got off and on 'em and rode 'em back and forth and around the car, yelling all the time. And there was a kind of a band with drums of all sizes on horses, with long horns and flutes and they made me deaf.

Well, after the riding there was a kind of a stunt with a lion. All of the boys that weren't too badly hurt got off of their horses and got onto some camels that didn't have any bridles or saddles at all and could only be guided by kicking 'em in the neck. Then some big men dragged out a cage with a mean looking lion in it.

With long poles, these men opened the front of the cage in a big circle of these boys on the camels. The riders didn't have any guns or poles or anything, just some bamboo things that Aunt Mary said were blow pipes and a lot of little darts like arrows to blow through these pipes.

Then the lion stood in the middle of them all, lashing his long tail with a duster on the end of it. The boys kicked their camels in the rump to make 'em go, and they rode all around him. He'd start at one to kill him, camel and all, and that one would put his peashooter to his mouth and shoot a little dart into the lion. And the lion roared and went kind of crazy with all those little poison darts in him. This went on till the lion got killed dead.

Then there was a bad fight between a cheetah (that is like a tiger) and a lot of things that looked like police dogs, but were wild. The cheetah killed three of the dog things, but the rest of them killed it, and it was as bloody as Uncle Ulrich on Saturday night in the butcher shop.

Even that Saturday after he had carried the dying doctor out of the shop and to the ambulance. That's when the whole town started looking for Willie, and we knew it was all up for him.

Because I'd been working at the beauty shop, I hadn't seen Ulrich for a long time until Pop came to the beauty shop with that piece of window cord in his hand. I ran out and went with him, and there was Uncle Ulrich carrying the doctor out to the ambulance.

Before we got there, the bell on the ambulance had stopped. As we ran up, we saw the crowd on the sidewalk, then Uncle Ulrich coming out carrying Dr. Harwood. Pop said just one word under his breath and he let the piece of window cord drop against my foot.

"Willie." That's all Pop said. And he was right, too, it was Willie, as the whole town knew in ten minutes.

But, as I say, that time Willie for once was in the right, though we couldn't know it then. We just thought he must have gone crazy to shoot poor Dr. Harwood. But of course we didn't know what really happened in the shop, because it wasn't till Sunday night we heard any side of it but Uncle Ulrich's.

Anyway, that's what these games reminded me of as I sat there beside the king watching his fourteen sons kill things.

I knew that this wild kind of dangerous sport was considered all right for people to do here, and manners is different in different places according to what kind of people has the manners. So I tried to look as if what happened here happened in Mattoon every time we gave a strawberry festival at the church.

When the games were over, I rode back in the car. It was night suddenly over the desert and cold. At the palace, great big torches flared in the wind to show us out of the car.

As soon as we got in the main hall, the king began pulling me towards a door, but I thought I'd had enough so I got away from him.

"What does he want to show me in there?" I asked Mr. Bosco.

"His machine," Mr. Bosco says, "he wants to show it to you."

The king began yelling to me to come on, but I got away and followed Aunt Mary up to our rooms.

"Good girl," says Aunt Mary, and we got ready for the banquet.

I was sure glad Aunt Mary had gotten my formals with long sleeves and a simple round neck line. Because I sure didn't trust those boys with any bare skin around.

I got into my white crepe dress with the silver oak leaves that made a kind of wreath around the neck, and the same embroidery made a kind of a girdle nice and flat and low down on the hips. The skirt was full at the bottom, but far from loose around the middle. There was one silver leaf on the bottom of each long sleeve. It was embroidered on a kind of a point that laid flat on the back of my hand. The skirt was long. I had silver slippers to go with it and a kind of a half wreath of metal leaves around the back of my hair under the knot, but reaching up on the sides. They had a border of white beads on 'em, so you could tell where my hair stopped and the silver leaves began.

So Aunt Mary and I left the girls that had oh-ed and ah-ed while we was dressing and we went out in a hall and down steps into a kind of a front yard. Only it wasn't one because the palace was all around it and it had a roof over most of it, but not all.

There was a fountain in the middle made out of pretty colored tiles making a splashing sound. The floor was a big design of black and white and yellow tiles. There were round-topped doors opening off of this place in all directions. It was all lit up with lanterns and looked pretty.

And there was Mr. Bosco in his shiny black suit. All he did for the banquet was to take off his hat and leave just his ears sticking out. He was smiling and seemed to think we looked pretty sharp.

Aunt Mary began to talk to him about Japan, and as I didn't know anything about Japan, I just wandered around looking at the flowers that seemed to spill out of everywhere and at the gold and silver and spotted fish, big enough to eat.

It seemed like I could hear machinery running, but I

couldn't be sure. Suddenly I saw a door open right by me, and a big man in a white nightgown beckoned with his big knotty hand for me to come in there.

I backed off towards Aunt Mary and Mr. Bosco pretty quick.

Then he opened the door a little wider, and this time I was sure I heard a machine running.

When he opened the door enough for me to see into the little room behind him, I knew darn well I had heard machinery, and my eyes bucked out like poached eggs. For there, in that little room, sitting all in white like a wicked old prophet out of a picture book was the old king working the machine, pushing something through it with his fingers.

His sleeves were thrown back so his arms would be free. And buzz, chuckachuck chuckachuck went this machine that I had been sure was going to be something to chop up people with. And for me to be seeing him working it so hard was just more than I could stand, so I let out a yell that must have woken up those sleepy wives all the way off in the harem. And no wonder I yelled when at last I saw his machine. It was a Singer sewing machine, exactly like Aunt Helga's that I learned to sew on from the day I was six years old.

I just yelled with laughing and couldn't stop. And even Aunt Mary looked a little scared—which she never did—and I knew she was afraid I'd hurt the old boy's feelings, so I tried harder to stop.

The funny thing about people that are different from you is how different they are. And instead of getting mad, the old boy opened up his big mouth that didn't have a tooth in it, except one away back, and he laughed louder than anything you ever heard. It boomed out like the town clock.

Well, the old king sat there and stopped sewing on his machine to laugh louder than I was laughing. Then he took his feet off of the treadles and came running out, still laughing.

People heard it, and doors busted open on the balconies all around, and some men that was a kind of an orchestra for the palace grabbed their instruments quick and begun to play.

They were good, too. Fast and hot licks, jiving and sending—mostly kind of out of tune, but cooking. And the old king took both of my hands and danced around me, holding on and laughing and bellering, "Palace Theater."

Then he led me into the little room. The others all crowded around in the doorway. Then suddenly he quit laughing and showed me the machine.

He had yards and yards of silk and satin and white stuff like cheese cloth and unbleached muslin, and he sat down like he was going to play the piano. He ran seams fast and then he ran 'em slow. When he got to the end of sewing two pieces together in a seam, he laid a piece of rose-colored ribbon flat on the seam and he sewed it down one side, and then, zip, right back up the other.

I never saw anybody more proud of what he was doing and I kept clapping for him. Finally, with a spurt of speed he shot around a curve and pulled up at the end of the seam and broke the thread and got up and did everything but take a bow.

Then everybody made a fuss about his little workout.

When things got a little quiet, I says to Mr. Bosco, "Ask him if he can work the attachments."

But Mr. Bosco didn't know what I meant, so I thought I'd find 'em, and I pushed the king out of the chair and started to sit down at the machine, but that was a mistake. The reason I knew it was a mistake was that all of the king's people made a kind of hushed groan.

So I stopped before I had even dusted the king's chair and leaned over and opened the bottom drawer. There were the attachments, all done up in their box, even with the tissue paper still wrapped around 'em.

So I unwrapped 'em and held 'em out to the king, but I could see from his face that he didn't know what they was for.

I wanted to go ahead and show our hosts and their king a thing or two, but I saw Aunt Mary's face watching, and I knew that you don't show kings up, not before their own gang anyway. So I attached the ruffler, and they all watched like I was lighting a giant firecracker with a very short fuse.

So I bowed to the old boy, to show respect, and then I reached up and took him by the shoulders and sat him down at his machine.

I stood behind him and put my arms over his shoulders and put a piece of wide gold-colored ribbon on. I turned the wheel till it took the first stitch, and I left the needle down to hold it.

Then I stepped aside and clapped my hands and says, "Attaboy."

He looked like he was scared, but he started pedaling. The machine began to do its stuff and when it came out a ruffle you'd have thought I had rose up off of the ground and floated through a hoop.

Well, when they had kind of got used to this miracle, I performed all the others that Mr. Singer ever thought of—the adjustable hemmer, the zigzag, the hemstitcher, the bias binder and the buttonholer.

But they liked the ruffler the best. And like Wo Baby, they thought what I said was the name of it: "Attaboy."

So, when the old king had ruffled about a yard of yellow ribbon, he put it around his turban and it looked pretty cute.

And, "Attaboy," he says, and everybody says, "Attaboy," and we all laughed and were very friendly.

Just then, on the other side of the fish fountain a big door opened and there was the prince, and, say, there he was, but what a difference. Behind him came the four sweets, but in green uniforms with gold braid and cords and tassels and, instead of their black hats, they had big things on their heads, as well as swords and white gloves.

And the prince, boy, he was something right out of Ali Babba and the Forty Thieves. He didn't look little now at all. He wore a tight coat like the one he loaned to me with long full skirts to the knees and slippers with silver embroidery and tight pants to the ankle and a head thing, wrapped on tight, with a little clothes brush in the front with a clip to hold it—diamonds it looked like—and a tight collar to the coat, buttoned up high at the neck. Everything he had on him was silver cloth or white, and on his chest were stars and little swords and square things lit up like State Street.

He stopped there in the light when he saw us across the open place.

"Don't he look beautiful?" says Aunt Mary, right by me. "He's like a child's dream of an Indian prince," she says, "those big eyes."

"Yes," I says, and I chuckled at the corny joke I had just thought of. "Aladdin," I says, "and his wonderful lamps."

Aunt Mary giggled soft and squeezed my hand.

Well, it seems there were four more other kings visiting in the palace that they had forgot to mention, but they came to the banquet all done up in silks, too. The guests at the banquet had on more drygoods than Marshall Field's basement and each one looked spiffier than the others.

The prince and me stood together on the top step, both all in white and silver as it happened, with the old king on the other side of me. Aunt Mary stood one step below us, and in a long line sat all but two of the king's sons looking grand, all washed and dressed up in the prettiest neglijays you ever saw.

The extra kings came in with their bodyguards and were presented to the king.

By now I had learned what to do when you're introduced. You shake hands with one—just one shake—then you let go and you hold up your right thumb against your right forefinger and you kiss the place where the thumb joins onto your hand. He does the same on his own hand, and that's all. The king kissed 'em all with a lot of little kisses on each cheek, them doing the same at the same time to him. But they don't do it to foreigners, and was I glad.

It was a real pretty scene like Dorothy Lamour, but without Bob or Bing.

The king took my one hand and the prince the other, and two other kings took Aunt Mary's hands, and in we went to get dinner.

It's no use trying to tell all about it. They had a way of eating that made it hard to keep the grease off of my best new formal, and there was more and more food. And then they brought out something huge and big, cooked whole, that I didn't know whether to be scared was the lion I'd seen earlier, but it tasted like giant chicken. There was rice by the mountain and gravy boats I could have swam in, and some of 'em nearly did. They had people with a basin to wash my hands, and they brought it to me right there, and I sure needed it.

There was music by the same rhythm boys that I told you about, and girls to dance to their music. Their dances sure said what they meant and the king's sons did a couple of double bumps just to show they knew what it did mean.

A pudding as big as a millstone and just about as heavy came in all afire. It tasted sweet but I didn't like it, and there was something around it that was just exactly like some pink fishing worms that used to visit us in Mattoon after a rain.

While the old king was deep in talk with the prince, one of the boys got out of his depth and he bit a dancing girl's stomach so deep you could see every tooth of his on her. She screeched, and the king looked around and all the boys fell over and laughed. So the king clapped his hands and two black men brought in a big monkey dressed just like this girl that his son had bit, and the king told the boy he'd have to bite the monkey right where he bit the girl.

He was scared to, but after a couple of tries he did it,

and the monkey bit him on the shoulder a lot worse than he had bitten the girl, because it bled, and everybody laughed like at the circus and didn't seem to care whether he died of blood poisoning or not.

Well, when the talk was over and we had drank enough strong coffee never to sleep again, the prince stood up and clapped his hands, and it got quiet. The doors opened, and there was Bill and Coo.

They came in all in white, carrying a blue velvet pillar between them. On it was what looked like a cube of ice out of a highball with an electric light in it, but it didn't have one in it, though it sure shined like it had. And the old king took it and I knew he had bought it, and it got passed around by Bill and Coo.

Well, I thought it must be about over. But no, the king stood up and clapped his hands and a lot of people came in with presents for everybody, especially me, and I perked right up.

Each of the boys got up and came over to the ones with the presents. The oldest brought me a string of pearls and put it around my neck. It was longer than the ones I got Millie at Carson's for three dollars. He looked at me and talked soft in his own language. Then each one did the same thing, till I had sixteen strings.

The pearls were heavy and very nice, but what I didn't know till Aunt Mary told me was that they were real pearls, and it's funny, but she said that real pearls are even better than Telca that I always thought was the best there was—better but not so pretty.

The king made a long speech and the prince made a long speech, and the music got louder and louder. There was a kind of sweet smoke in the air from some vases that had rubber tubes attached to 'em that the boys kept smoking. This smoke was heavy and perfumed and smelled like Mass at Saint Stephen's. I don't know how it happened but I do know that when I woke up, everybody was looking at me and laughing.

The king gave me a thing for around my ankle with green sets in it and I said thank you to everybody. Aunt Mary and I said goodnight and walked out of the room very dignified.

In bed I could still hear the party going, with yelps and shrieks and hollering from the boys. I could hear the noise even in my dreams. Then it was time to get up and go to India where I hoped people wouldn't make so much noise and they didn't.

When we went to where the plane was, standing there ready to fly, all the Soodans for miles around came to see us off. They came on camels and horses and mules and their feet to see us fly.

Mr. Bosco was there watching the sweets load the gold that the prince had gotten for the ice cube, and some men with long rifles were standing around.

We were waiting for the king to come to say goodbye, and little did we know what we were to see when he did come. Of course it wasn't so funny to anybody but Aunt Mary and me, and we wouldn't have laughed for anything. But it sure took control.

All of the boys came galloping up on their horses and they smarted off all over the desert, and if I turned away while one of 'em was standing on his head at a dead gallop around the plane, all the others would laugh at him.

"Nice boys," says Mr. Bosco, "they love you very much."

"But where's the oldest, the one with the black beard parted in the middle, the one that caught me yesterday when I slid off of Wo Baby?"

"You'll see," said Mr. Bosco. "He's going to do something. It is a secret."

"Then how do you know it?" I says.

"I know everything," he says.

"Where's the king?" I says. "He's late."

"He will come," he says, "but he's very busy."

"That's a lot of gold there," I says.

"We are taking it back to the prince's brother," he says.

"It must be quite a lot," I says, "all this plus what he got for the stuff in America. What's his brother going to do with so much?"

"Can you keep a secret?" says Mr. Bosco. "You will not tell Aunt Mary?" he says.

"No," I says.

"You are going to be a princess, so I will tell you. Prince's big brother," he said, "wants much money. The prince goes to get it. Big brother, he loves the Japanese very much because the Japanese have much money. Big brother has a big state with much flat land—very nice, no jungle. The Japanese like flat land very much—it's nice for war."

"You mean they want to fight the war right there on his state?" I says. "Who with?"

"Oh, no," he says and he laughed. "You see this plane? It can't land on the sea and it can't land in the jungle. But it will land fine on flat land."

By this time the gold was all loaded.

"Tell me some more," I says.

"Halla Bandah is coming," he says. "Don't tell him what I told you. Don't tell Aunt Mary, either."

I looked to where she was sitting in the plane, writing.

"Why not tell her?" I says. "She's my aunt."

"Maybe aunt," he says, "maybe not."

And there was the prince, standing there beside us in his regular black suit, looking little again and kind of pitiful.

We walked towards the plane.

"Did you know," I asked the prince, "that the oldest boy of the king is going to do something?"

"He might," he says.

"Is that why you've got these men with the long guns standing all around?" I says.

"These men with long guns," he says, "they are his men."

"Have your sweet got any guns on 'em?" I says.

"Yes," he says, "but four to how many?"

Then everything seemed to be about ready, except that the king hadn't come to say goodbye and the oldest son was still missing.

"I wouldn't think," I says, "that the king's son would come up and steal back some gold that his father give to you in a fair trade."

"He wouldn't," he says. "We have other treasures besides gold," and his eyes looked at me soft.

"But how do you know he's going to do something?" I says.

"Your Aunt Mary told me," he says.

I looked at her sitting there quietly, writing in her little book. And just then we heard three big bangs.

It wasn't guns. It was about twenty drummers, sitting on their horses, that had rode up in a long line. They had two big drums, one on each side of each horse, and with the palms of their hands they had all hit on all forty drums all at once.

It was a kind of a salute, I guess, for at that minute the king's big open job of a car come sailing up with the old king standing up in the back seat. The wind was blowing his red beard way out on each side. He stood there like something noble in the Elk's parade, and of all the things I saw in all my travels, the sight of him was the one thing I couldn't never possibly forget. He must have been busy all night. For, believe me, he looked like Mae West's pincushion.

He must have ruffled a hundred yards of ribbon on Mr. Singer's sewing machine, all colors, and he had it fluttering all over him everywhere.

There were ruffles on his turban, yellow and pink, till it looked like an old fashioned boudoir cap. And he had rosettes—yellow and blue and green and red—stuck on all over his burnoose and on the sleeves of that nightgown thing they wear under the burnoose. Oh, he had ruffles just all over him and even flying out behind him, flapping and fluttering in the wind.

The car stopped and everything was quiet and the king stood there with a serious frown. Then he made a bow to me, touching his forehead and his heart. And then he raised up and yelled at me in his big bull voice.

"Palace Theater," he yelled, and, "Palace Theater," they all yelled right back at him.

He was so sweet like a pleased kid in a masquerade costume, that king or no king, I ran across to his car and climbed up on the running board and kissed him on each cheek.

And, "Attaboy," they all yelled.

And, "Attaboy," he yelled again.

Just then there was a great galloping across the sand and there, riding up, was the oldest son with about twenty men on horses. And they all had smallish bags of something slung across their saddles, one bag on each side. And he made his horse rear up, and then he stood up in the stirrups and made a long loud speech right at the prince.

Halla Bandah Rookh stood on the top of the steps that led down from our plane. And he listened to the speech.

I saw the four sweets and the pilot and the copilot all with a hand in their pocket and we all stood still till this man got through speaking.

When he had said his say, he took a bag off of the horse next to him and throwed it on the ground at the prince's feet and it made a clinking sound. And then he'd throw another bag and wait. And each time this son of a king throwed down a bag onto the pile he'd yell out how much was in it.

I never saw so many people and so many horses so quiet in my life. There was just the clink of the bag on the sand and then the yell of how much, then everything quiet.

Finally all the bags was off of the horses on the ground. And all of the men with long guns was in one big bunch.

Then the prince walked slowly down the steps and stood on the ground. And the king's son got off his horse and somebody led it away. And there they stood, facing one another.

When the prince spoke it was quiet but firm as a rock. He said a long sentence. Then he stopped. The king's son looked down at him and explained something back. Then the horsemen eased their horses a step closer.

I was still on the running board of the king's car, and he, like all the rest of us, was listening and watching.

Of course I couldn't understand a word, but I knew it was mighty important stuff, whatever it was.

Well, the king's son said his last word and anybody could see and hear, too, that it was a pretty dangerous word. But the prince walked over to him and said a plain, "No."

Then the men on their horses drew up their bridles and shifted their guns, and this was IT, and everybody knew it.

Then suddenly, there was Aunt Mary stepping out of the door of the plane onto the top step. "Wait a minute," she says, and was I glad of three words that I could understand. But those was the only ones I could, for what she said next was to the prince and it was in French and at the end she pointed at the king.

The prince listened with his back nearly to her, still facing the king's son.

When she stopped, he turned to the king and asked him a question in his language.

The king said something that meant yes.

Now Aunt Mary had a kind of smile on her lips and she told the prince in French what to say.

Then he took a short step toward the car and in a louder voice he said a short quick thing, just a flat statement, and everybody took a short quick breath and they all waited for what the king would say.

Well, they didn't have to wait long. The old boy barked out an order that would have made that statue of General Grant in the town square at home jump to attention to obey it, and believe me, those men on their horses dropped their guns and backed their horses away and did just like their old king ordered them to do.

The king got out of the car and then he barked out another order, and they all jumped off of their horses, and some of 'em held all the bridles, and the rest of 'em fell to and began clearing away that pile of money bags and carried 'em back double-quick and hung 'em back across the saddles.

The king's oldest son pleaded with his old father, but his pop said, "Nothing doing." And the king took me by the hand and led me like we was dancing the lancers over to the steps and we all said goodbye. The other sons that had just been watching everything that had happened came up, crowding and yelling, and we got in the plane. Our steps were pulled up, the motors roared and we beat it for India.

CHAPTER ELEVEN

IN THE PLANE I DIDN'T think I had better ask any questions till we got settled down some.

Aunt Mary sat by me, thinking, but still with that little smile around her mouth.

"Hi, water lily," she says.

"Hi, wise old fish," I says right back.

"Well," she says, "you ought to feel pretty flattered."

"How?" I says.

"He was trying to buy you," she says, "for a wife."

"What was in those bags?" I says.

"Gold," she says. "It was like an auction. You see when the prince said no, the king's son offered more and more till he thought he had offered enough."

"Then what happened?"

"The prince still said no."

"What happened then?" I says.

"Then the king's son said what in Soodanese meant 'Okay, prince, I'll take her anyhow. Try and stop me.'"

"Was that when you butted in?" I says.

"I thought I had better," she says and she patted my hand. "I didn't feel like I wanted to lose you, you being the nicest niece I ever had."

"Thanks," I says, and I got her to tell me just what she had said to the prince and what he had said to the old king and how we had got away.

Well, what she had told the prince was to ask the king: if this son did take me by force or bought me, wasn't it one of their customs for the king to give his new daughter-in-law whatever she asked for as a wedding present? So the prince asked him and the king said yes.

Well, after Aunt Mary had tricked the king into saying it like that, she told the prince to tell the boys that there was just one thing I would ask for, and that was the last thing in the world that old boy would part with.

For she knew that before he would have given up that Singer sewing machine, he would have seen that son and all his other sons turned into camel boys, and he'd have seen all his wives and dancing girls go to someone else.

"So, what could he do," said Aunt Mary, chuckling, "but lead you to the plane and say goodbye quick. But oh, my dear," says Aunt Mary, "wouldn't you trade everything you own, including sixteen strings of pearls and your emerald anklet and even your B.V.D.'s for that picture of that old king riding up in all those ruffles like a circus clown on a mule."

I had some problems to think out and thinking things out is something you've got to get quiet to do, so I did. Up to now, I didn't think much about us being at war, except Jeff was getting in it to be a soldier.

I don't know much about wars, not having been there at the last one, or the Spanish American one—which Pop was in—or the Civil War that my Swede grandfather came over from the other side to be at.

So now here was another one, and me about to go to
where some of it was to be at. For it seemed like the
Japanese were right by India, which I didn't know—I
thought it was nearer to California, which goes to show
that I never ought to have left that geography book
behind the Girls' john.

I had to get what thoughts I could together and I
hoped when I did, they'd fit. But when I did, they didn't.
Well, I had to think it out, so I kept thinking.

The prince wouldn't sell me for a pile of gold. Also
he had sure risked his life to save me, and that always
makes the girl in the movie turn her eyelashes towards
the hero and say "I didn't dream you cared," just before
the fadeout.

Aunt Mary was quite a woman, which I had already
guessed, but I'd never seen her do her stuff before.
How had she known the king's oldest son had been up
to something?

Then there was Mr. Bosco. What about him?

And was the prince only getting money for his
brother to give to the Japanese, or was there more to that
oath of being blood brothers than I knew about?

And that was all I could think out right now, but it
sure made me pretty tired.

Well, we flew over Ethiopia where that man with the
beard and the umbrella used to live, but didn't now
anymore on account of Mussolini.

Then, with some stops, we flew along beside a lot of
water. Land on the left, water on the right. It was all too
mixed up for me, so Mr. Bosco quit trying to teach me
where we was at, and was I glad.

I thought it was better just to learn about things that could do me some good, and what use were all those names of people and places that nobody I know were hardly going to believe, even if I were foolish enough to try to make 'em believe, that I had ever been there.

Then the prince came and sat with me, and I was afraid this was it. And it was, but not like I was afraid it was. Because all I had to do was listen mostly.

"I'm so sorry," he says, "about everything back there."

"Oh, that's all right," I says, "and thank you for not selling me."

"What?" he says. "Oh, never, never."

"Thank you, all the same," I says. "I know how you must need money. If you go around like this from door to door selling your jewelry, you must need it bad. So when you could have got such a big pile of gold for just selling me, it might have been a temptation."

"No, no," he says, "I would never do that."

"Well, anyway," I says, "if it hadn't have been for your kindness, I might be spending tonight rubbing henna leaves in that black beard and so I'm much obliged," I says.

"Now we come soon to Bombay," he says. "Bombay is in India," he says. "And after Bombay we go to Calcutta," he says. "And after Calcutta we go to my house."

"That's fine," I says, "and then you'll see your brother. And then you and him can do what you both planned with all the money. Share and share alike."

"No," he says, "no share for me. It is all for him if I can make him take it. But if I cannot make my brother take this money it will break my father's heart."

"Why?" I says.

"Because if I cannot, then it will be too late for me to save my brother, and what he does, I will do." And he touched the little lotus flower button in his lapel.

"Listen," I says, "that button is a part of your oath with your brother."

"It is," he says.

"And do you really believe that if your brother does something bad—that you don't want to be mixed up in—you ought to let your father think you are just as deep in it as him?"

"You do not understand," he says.

"Answer me just one question," I says, "and for one minute, forget about the oath."

"Ask," he says.

"Do you love the Japanese?" I says.

"No," he says.

"But if your brother is up to something…?"

"Maybe he is not," he says, "or even if he is, maybe I give him more money."

"You mean more than the Japanese give him?"

"My brother was always a good boy when we were young."

"Is that when you began wearing the same button-hole?" I says.

"Yes," he says, "in the temple, in front of priests, we swear."

"Now listen, you poor kid," I says. "You made your bargain in good faith, but what's bad in your bargain is that your podner let you down. And now you're going to try to buy him back from being bad."

"I must try," he says.

"All right," I says. "Try your best, and then if you fail, break the oath. Break it so you will feel free."

"Maybe he will listen," he says. "Maybe a friend will help me."

"Mr. Bosco?" I says.

"Maybe," he says.

"Tell me," I says, "what has Mr. Bosco got to do with all this business?"

"How do you mean?" he says.

"Well, your family," I says, "seems to be pretty well-to-do. And," I says, "it seems funny, him being such a poor little man with only one shiny suit, even if he does seem pretty educated in a good many languages. Does he mean to get a cut-in with your brother?"

"A cut?" he says.

"Does Mr. Bosco get a share of this money or does he want your brother to help his country, or what?"

He smiled.

"Mr. Bosco," he says (only he didn't call him that), "Mr. Bosco is one of the richest men in Burma—like Rockefeller."

Well, that stopped me I can tell you.

Pretty soon Mr. Bosco himself came back from up where they run the plane, and he took off his little hat.

"Excuse me please," he says, "the pilot asks humbly to speak with the prince."

So the prince excused himself and went up there and Mr. Bosco sat down.

"Hello," he says.

"Hello," I says. "Tell me this," I says. "Was you going

to stand there on that desert like at a cattle auction," I says, "and let the king's son buy me right before your eyes?"

"I was waiting," he says, with a little bow, "till the bidding got up to what you were worth, then I would have bid. No use bidding chicken feed," he says.

"Listen, Mr. Bosco," I says, "where is Burma at?"

"India there," he says and he put his left forefinger on one knee, "Burma right next door." He put his right forefinger on the other knee.

"Is it in Japan?"

"Not yet," he says, "not yet. Some bad men in my country, they think it is so, but not yet."

We stopped next at some place very foreign looking, I forget where. There were boats for hire (because it was on the water) and they were very pretty. The tassels and seat covers were nice but not too clean. There was a very ugly man with one eye that sailed one and I didn't think the sweets liked him.

But I got Aunt Mary to come along for the boat ride on this gulf—Persian Gulf I think somebody said—so the three of us could talk instead of just the prince and me. But Aunt Mary made friends with the one-eyed gorilla and he taught her how to sail, so that left him and me together and he started right in.

"I had a very sad childhood," he says. "I was not happy. I ran away from the English school. My brother is better educated. He is tall, my brother, and very handsome. I am short and not handsome. I love my brother. You see what I do for him. To old king in Soodan I sell a diamond he's wanted for fifteen years. So I take it and sell to him, and now I am afraid to come home."

"Why?" I says. "Are you afraid of him?"

"Yes," he says, "but if you like my state, I will be glad. I want my father to see you, you are so beautiful. My father wants very much for me to have a wife," he says. "I want very much that you like my father, that you like me. I know the many difference between us."

I thought he meant language so I says, "Don't worry about that." He went on.

"Your religion, it is not my religion. How do you feel about that? Your religion is sacred to you, as mine is to me."

"Religion ain't so sacred to me," I says, "whether it's one kind or another. I guess it's a good thing to have some, but one kind or another, I can't see much difference. I was confirmed in Saint Stephens, but the incense made me sick. I got kind of a weak stomach, see? So then I went to the Lutherans, and I guess you can be good there same as in a cathedral—it sure ain't as pretty, but the air is better. I guess your church ain't no more different from Lutherans than Lutherans are from the Jewish church. I knew a girl who went to that church, or synagogue as they call it. And she was as nice a girl as I ever met. I guess God don't go around saving just one little bunch from all the kinds. One is as good as another if it makes you nice and keeps you from hurting people that can't defend themselves. That's the important thing. Does your church teach you that?"

"You don't seem to realize," he says, "you would call my church heathen."

"Listen," I says, "I've seen a lot of heathens setting up in churches in new Easter hats, don't think I haven't. You're no heathen. You're kind and polite and good," I says.

"I am glad you do not mind," he says.

"Excuse me," I says, "but if I ain't mistaken you was kind of proposing to me just now."

"Proposing?" he says.

"Asking me to marry you, if your pop thinks I'm Okay."

"Asking you that, yes, but I do not know how in English."

"Oh, you're doing all right," I says, "but we've got to talk about that. You can't do that," I says. "You don't know nothing about me."

"You are good," he says.

"Lots of girls are good that ain't good girls," I says. "You can't go halfway around the world and pick up a girl selling cigarettes in Butch's Café on the West Side of the Loop in Chicago and say, 'Hi, Toots, how'd you like to be a princess?'"

"I did not say that," he says.

"Listen," I says. "I know darn well that in your country, you haven't got any little friends selling cigarettes that you'd ask your pop to pass on. I look nice now," I says, "in what Aunt Mary bought me, but if you'd seen me in what I've got back in my room in Chicago, you wouldn't have gotten fooled into forgetting that you're a prince," I says, "and that I'm a girl that's worked for her living and will have to go on doing it when she gets back. Which mustn't be too long," I says, "or I'll have to start all over again. And if you knew what the smell of a beauty parlor does to my insides, you sure wouldn't want me to have to go back to that," I says.

"You are good," was all he said, and big tears came up into his eyes.

I couldn't say more then but when I was back in the plane I tried to think some more, but nothing much came of it.

Like I always do when I can't seem to think, I started planning. Only I couldn't do that very well because I didn't know where I was, how far it was from home or how I was going to get back there. So I did what I do when I can't either think or plan: I started remembering. That was something I didn't much like to do, but it couldn't be helped sometimes.

I remembered Pop and me sitting in the kitchen, him drinking a cup of coffee. Sunday night, it was, after he had worked all day on that scabbing job for Uncle Ulrich. Then he'd had to work all Sunday night nearly to get it done because we had to interrupt it to get him to the coroner's inquest on Dr. Harwood.

And there was Uncle Ulrich's gun at the inquest but Willie's fingerprints. Uncle Ulrich said, yes, it had been Willie's doing, that he just came into the shop while Dr. Harwood had been buying something. Uncle Ulrich testified that the boy just seemed to have a grudge, he guessed that's what it was, on account of the doctor giving evidence that was sure to go against Willie at his trial about the McComber girl.

So this night Pop had to stay late to finish building the killing pen for Uncle Ulrich, and I sat up in the kitchen to wait for him and keep the coffee hot. And I could hear Aunt Helga rocking in her room and Uncle Ulrich snoring in his room.

And then Pop come in the back way, so thin and pale under his eyes.

I made him drink his coffee and then we just sat there in the kitchen together, and there wasn't much we could say. But I was thinking, there was my brother hiding out somewhere, and every radio on every motorcycle in the state saying his name and age and what he had on. And Pop thinking the same. Then all of a sudden there Willie was at the window. He came inside the door and moved to the corner. I pulled the blind down just like I'd seen sisters or wives or mothers or sweethearts do in a thousand second features.

Willie wanted to talk to us, that's why he'd taken the chance and come back. He told us he went to the shop Saturday, going in the back way, to beg Uncle Ulrich to tell the truth about Darlene when his trial came up. And while he was begging Uncle Ulrich, somebody came past the window, and Uncle Ulrich said, "Get out of sight, quick." Willie got behind the end of the big refrigerator room. Dr. Harwood came in, but the doctor started thanking Uncle Ulrich for the help he'd been to him getting off. Uncle Ulrich tried to stop him so Willie wouldn't hear. But Willie heard all right.

And he said it all came over him how he was being framed by Uncle Ulrich, so he took the gun that always stays on a little shelf by the cash drawer and he pointed it at Uncle Ulrich. The next thing he knew the doctor was on the floor and Uncle Ulrich was bending over him, so Willie got out the back door.

Well, I gave Willie quick what money I had in my purse, handed him a sandwich and made him finish his coffee. He kissed me, and then he grabbed Pop and kissed him, too. I knew Willie would go now and maybe get away and we'd never see him again, and I was glad.

So I put the light out and I opened the door for him quietly, and then he ran out of the door right into the arms of Sheriff O'Conner.

So now on the plane over the Arabian Sea I just watched the glow of the sunset till it was night. And there was Coo with cool little slices of pickled melon that was a little sweet and a little salty and I says, "Hello, Coo." And then there was Bill with strong black tea with mint in it and little crackers that tasted like rat-trap cheese, and I says, "Hello, Bill," and he laughed in a squeak. And I settled back as the lights came on and the curtains were drawn and I felt rested and at home with these people that were so nice to me and wouldn't sell me, even for a fortune. I nibbled melon and sipped tea and slid down in my seat and slept like a baby till it was time for dinner.

That night when I was in bed I got to thinking again, and the more I tried not to, the more I did. Finally I stuck my head into Aunt Mary's berth and there she was writing with a little pen that had a little light on it.

"Aunt Mary," I says, "I got to talk."

"Talk away," says Aunt Mary, and her little light went out.

"Well," I says, "for the first time in my life I wish I had studied my geography better."

"Why?" she says.

"Well, at least I would know where I am at."

"The pilot's got a very stylish map you could study,

or I've got a smaller one. But if you're the girl I think you are," she says, "you'll be happier if you don't look at any map at all."

"What's Burma?" I says.

"It's a country."

"Are there Japanese people in it?"

"Quite a lot."

"Is there a town called Nagasaki in it?"

"No," she says, "that's in Japan."

"That's what I thought."

"Go on," she says.

"Well," I says, "Mr. Bosco says he lives in Japan," I says, "in a town called Nagasaki, but the prince told me Mr. Bosco is the richest man in Burma. How can a Japanese man that lives in Nagasaki be the richest man in Burma? And anyway I never want to worry you, but what are we doing traveling with a man from an enemy country," I says, "two of whose countrymen were bluffing Washington while a lot of other Japanese countrymen were bombing the hell out of our Pearl Harbor," I says, and I was sure surprised to find I was about to cry.

"Listen, dear child," Aunt Mary says, "I am an American."

"So what?" I says, sniffling.

"I am an American, but I've lived and worked most of my life in England and Europe," she says. "And Mr. Bosco is like that, too. He's a Burmese."

"He's a what?" I says.

"A Burmese who's lived for many years in Japan and who travels to South America once a year to look after his interests," she says.

"You mean Mr. Bosco is not Japanese?"

"Mr. Bosco is not Japanese," she says. "Why didn't you ask me long ago, or ask him?"

"I don't know," I said, and I was so glad Mr. Bosco wasn't from Japan that I forgot all the other things I had wanted to ask Aunt Mary.

As I left her, she patted my hand. "We will soon have found out everything I came over from London to America to find out," she says, "and I could never have done it at all without you."

CHAPTER TWELVE

WELL, WE GOT TO BOMBAY all right, after stopping at a couple of places, and I knew this was India as soon as I saw it. But I didn't know before how many English there were in India till I got there and saw.

I asked Aunt Mary, and she said England had to watch her step in India but I didn't know until later what she meant.

What a place! It was a mixture of clean and dirty, of parlors and cowsheds—a lot of cowsheds. For it seemed these round-shouldered cows were sacred, sort of, and they got treated better than anybody. Nobody could drive 'em or housebreak 'em. It sure showed me what Aunt Mary meant about what England had to watch.

In India there were many poor people and a lot of very rich people. I saw people carry things that I didn't think a mule would be able to.

My butterflies all went crazy and never stopped fluttering hardly a minute in any of the Indian cities I was in. They were only quiet when we got to the country where the prince and his papa and his brother all lived.

But first we went to Calcutta.

The prince and Mr. Bosco went off somewhere as

soon as we got there, I guess to the bank of the little old London lady. Aunt Mary told me the Bank of England is called the little old lady of Thread Needle Street, which is sure silly. And it's not because it's English, but because anybody ought to know that a great big bank sounds better as the First National or like that, than the little old lady of anything.

There were English newspapers in Calcutta and the war was awful.

Aunt Mary had to see a lot of English people all the time. Whenever we started out to a bazaar, we always ended up with some Englishmen that looked at me with eyes like bad little boys that would sure like to start something if their mothers hadn't made 'em promise not to.

When she was busy, Aunt Mary would find a nice young man with a face like a pink-and-white angel to talk to me so she could go in the other office with some other Englishman, and the young men they left me with seemed pretty silly I thought, never saying what they meant.

If they wanted to tell me about five thousand of the poor dying of the plague, or a riot with a lot of one kind of people cutting the hearts out of a lot of another kind of people of a different religion, they'd laugh and tell it, and then they'd say, "Rather a tidy little tea party that," or "Quite a neat bit of a show, what?"

At first, I got kind of out of patience with 'em, but I soon found out that they were just being English and that's why they did it.

It's just that they were scared to say something to me that was so horrible I would never forget it, so they'd say, "A priceless little quadrille if I ever saw one." Those were the top-notch English that did that. The Cockneys are different, as I found out from one but I'll tell that when I come to it.

As I say, the English were like that, but at the time I'd never met one, so I had to get to understand 'em.

Once I got to know 'em, I found that they'd die for me, still talking that way, as if it was all just a "tidy little show, what?" Too shy to ever come out and say it like they mean it, and that's what makes England England, Aunt Mary says.

I know now she was right, because not two weeks later Captain Sir Rodney Carmichael—with his arm nearly cut off—sat with me in a little rubber boat somewhere not far from Australia and he had sure saved my life because whatever swimming Pop had taught me was no good to me in the Indian Ocean. Captain Sir Rodney Carmichael's left arm wasn't hardly on him at all, and I stopped the blood the way I had learned to when I had tried to help Willie become a Boy Scout, though he never did.

Well, after I stopped it with nearly all of the dress I had left on me twisted on a piece of the propeller that I found floating there, we sat in that little rubber square doughnut, in the broiling sun, and him laughing at what I said when I tried to talk about what was to become of us, if anything.

It's hard to believe it but he said it just like they all do, "After this jolly little picnic, we surely know each other well enough for you to begin calling me Roddy, what?"

So I knew Aunt Mary had been right, they can sure take it.

Well, that's the kind of Englishmen that gave me a dish of tea in Calcutta and they thought I was pretty funny and laughed a lot at what I said, and me at them just as much.

Finally at night we got to the prince's house in his own state. It was just like something I had seen once and hadn't ever forgotten. It was an old picture that got revived called *The Thief of Bagdad.*

There was a white palace in that. And here it was in the moonlight. It was as clean and quiet as I had hoped India might be before I saw it.

People came out and hugged Bill and Coo. And the prince and Mr. Bosco went off and I was sure they went to see the prince's brother.

Aunt Mary seemed nervous—it was the first time I had ever seen her like that. We sat in the shade of a big flat umbrella made of a flat piece of painted stone and drank something cool and sweet and she told me she was stumped. And for the first time she told me right out what we were really doing here. It sure gave me a turn.

We were here to watch the prince. That's why we had come on this long trip, because even though Aunt Mary had gotten to like him nearly as much as I did, she had to watch him and report on him because that was her business. And I found out she wasn't working for Mr. Hoover at all.

She never came right out and told me who she was working for, and maybe I never would have known if Lady Burroughs hadn't have told me what she did about the whole thing. But we didn't meet Lady Burroughs until we went to the prince's father's house and that wasn't until the prince and Mr. Bosco came back from going to see his brother. They hadn't been able to see his brother because he wasn't home, and nobody would tell 'em where the prince's brother was at.

And now Aunt Mary was nervous because she had found out from some English friends she had had a get-together with in Calcutta that the prince was sure in deep, and the English kind of had the stuff on him, and his brother, too. They were both, it seemed, pretty bad boys, she said, and even though we had got to like him she was mighty afraid that Sir Gerald would do some arresting, and pretty quick. In fact she said she knew Sir Gerald meant to arrest the prince at his father's house.

"Who's Sir Gerald?" I says.

"He's an old friend of mine," she says, "and he knows more about India than Gandhi does. Gerald is the typical fuddy-duddy," she says, "but when it comes to action he always surprises me by being a man of it."

"Of what?" I says.

"Of action," she says, and then her eyes got gentle and she put her hand on mine. "Listen, child," she says, "you've done a fine job, and I am deeply fond of you," she says, "and what's worrying me now is that you are going to be hurt."

"How?" I says.

"This is a hard-boiled game," she says, "and I know you have grown to like Halla Bandah, and so have I. So be prepared," she says, "for a shock when we get to his father's palace. For anything Sir Gerald does will have to be done quick, or it won't work. This is a military secret. But I know if I tell you it's safe."

"Sure," I says, but my heart felt tight and cold.

Well, like I said, Mr. Bosco and the prince finally got back, but the prince went right off again in a car, and Aunt Mary and me had dinner alone together.

The moon sure made the front yard of the palace look like a picture postcard. The front yard was about the size of Humboldt Park, and when Aunt Mary went to her room to write, I walked out in it. I walked farther and farther down some steps with stone railings cut out like lace, and finally I got to a little hill, and on the top of it was a little house that wasn't really a house because there weren't any walls to it, just a marble floor and a fountain and a roof.

So I climbed up the little hill by some broad flat steps, and then I saw there was somebody in the little house, and I started to go away again.

"Don't go," says a voice that I knew.

"Mr. Bosco," I says, "what are you doing out here?"

"I am looking at the moon," he says. "What are you doing?"

"Oh, Mr. Bosco," I says, "I'm sure glad to see you."

"Me, too," he says.

"I want to ask your pardon," I says.

"Granted," he says.

"No, wait," I says. "I thought you were from Japan."

"Granted," says Mr. Bosco.

"Listen," I says, "I know the prince and his brother are in cahoots," I says.

"Where is that?" he says.

"That means they must do everything together, see?"

"That is English?" he says.

"Maybe it's Swedish, but that's what it means," I says.

"I see," he says, "you are right, they are in cahoots."

"And you know what they are up to," I says.

"I only know," he says, "that the prince's brother has many men. All of his soldiers make a fine orchard. Many men made for prince's brother a beautiful big orchard, but they cut down all the trees and made a great flat place, big, for orchard, but no fruit trees in sight. What kind of trees do you think they're gonna be?"

"Maybe," I says, "nice cherry trees, like what we had in Washington. But I guess by now they changed the name of these trees, like German fried potatoes in the last war. You guess maybe that's what the prince's brother is waiting for? Nice cherry trees from way off?"

"Granted," says Mr. Bosco.

"Listen," I says, "when are we going to visit the prince's father? He said he was going to take me."

"Tomorrow night we go to dinner," he says.

"Tomorrow night?" I says. "Will the prince's brother be there, too?"

"I don't think so," says Mr. Bosco. "Since we got here, Halla Bandah has looked everywhere for his brother. He has gone now again to try and find him."

"I wish I could ask if you know a lot of things, Mr. Bosco."

"Better not to ask if I know what you know," he says, "because you promised Aunt Mary not to tell."

"Mr. Bosco," I says, "you're wonderful."

"Granted," he says and off he went.

I went back to the palace, and there was Aunt Mary strolling up and down in the moonlight.

"Hello," she says.

"Hello," I says, but I didn't feel like talking and pretty soon we went to bed.

My room had a high narrow window with stone lace around the top and a balcony outside. When I was nearly asleep I heard a car slide on its brakes and stop. I listened, and the car went away. Everything was as quiet as I had hoped India would be when I was in Africa. And then I heard a match strike outside of the window. Then it was quiet again like before.

I couldn't stand it so I got up and put on my slippers and my wrapper and I tiptoed over to the window. The balcony kept me from looking straight down, so I stepped out on it so I could. And there down below me stood the prince smoking a cigarette with his back to me.

"Hello," I says quietly, "is anything the matter?"

"Yes," he says, "I was wishing you were awake."

"Well, you got your wish," I says.

"Can we talk?" he says.

"I'll be right down," I says, and I went in and twisted my hair up and put on stockings and shoes. My wrapper was white crepe and had a lot of wraparound and a belt. So I just opened the door and went down the steps. He was standing at the bottom waiting for me.

"I want to talk where no one will hear," he says.

"I know a place," I says.

"Good," he says. And I went outside and started for the little house where I had met Mr. Bosco, and the prince caught up and walked with me till we got there and sat down.

"You are wise," he says. "You have taught me very much."

"How?" I says.

"You gave me words of wisdom about my brother. You say the oath can be broken."

"I didn't mean to butt in," I says.

"You are wise, like my father," he says. "Tomorrow we go to see my father."

"Who will be there?" I says.

"Some English," he says, "will be there. Lady Burroughs," he says, "and her husband."

"What's his name?" I says.

"General Sir Gerald Burroughs," he says. And in my stomach just one little butterfly begun to flutter.

"Did you find your brother?" I says.

"I could not," he says, "but I have sent him a message to meet me tomorrow night at the house of my father."

"Golly," I says.

"What?" he says.

"Nothing."

"On the way to my father's house I would like you to see the temple," he says.

"I'd like to," I says.

"I do not want your Aunt Mary to come with us."

"That's all right," I says. "Is Mr. Bosco going to your father's place?"

"Yes, he is a great friend of my father."

"Could Aunt Mary go in another car with him?"

"If you think she will not think it is not polite."

"I'll fix it," I says. "I want to go with you to the temple. Is it your church?"

"It is like that. It was at the temple that we made the oath, my brother and me."

"I'll go with you," I says.

"Thank you," he says. "You see my country," he says. "You like it?"

"I like your house," I says, "and I like you."

He was so sort of pitiful I felt like I wanted to say something that would please him. I had been very careful not to let him see that I was a little overwhelmed by this country, especially the cows.

The next morning I told Aunt Mary what I was going to do. So she and Mr. Bosco started off about the middle of the afternoon in a car together, and the prince and me likewise.

"You know," I says, as we were driving away from our first stop, which turned out to be what he called his orchid swamp. "Once I took Martine McCullough to our church—I mean Saint Stephens—and she was a Baptist so she didn't know how to bless herself, or to show respect to the altar when she crossed the church, or to hit her chest for mea culpa, or that girls without a hat were supposed to wear handkerchiefs over girls' heads, or nothing. I'm telling you this because you know I have never been to a temple before so if I don't do right it ain't lack of respect."

"Thank you," he said.

"Are you just going there to show it to me, or do you want to say your prayers after being away so long?"

"Both," he says. "The wise men of the temple gave me their blessing when I went away. Now I go to tell them I am back safe," he says.

"That's fine," I says.

"And perhaps for other reasons, too," he says.

We were driving off of the road through a good road into a jungle. And it was kind of a place where we got quiet, and even the two men that was driving us went slowly and we just floated through that dark green place.

All of a sudden we turned sharp and I was knocked breathless, for there in front of us was a statue of a lady, big enough to scare Dracula. She was a stone lady about the size of the courthouse in Springfield. She looked peaceful and quiet, and there was no light hardly under the trees and vines and stuff.

They stopped the car and we got out and they drove the car around the back of her, like going around a building, and there we stood in front of that huge big lady. She didn't look like our Virgin of course, but she was calm and quiet and I could sure feel how they must feel about her.

I just stood there looking up at her, and while I was, a little streak of sunlight broke through those big trees from somewhere and fell across her face and I saw there was a little smile on it. All of a sudden from the damp shade of the jungle there came up a great swarm of yellow butterflies and they fluttered up into that sunlight and once around this virgin's head and away off up into the sky.

The prince looked at me.

"She's beautiful," I says.

"It is here," he says, "on this spot that I made the oath with my brother."

"Then it's right here that you could break it," I says.

"That is why I have come here," he says, "and that

is why I wanted you to come with me. I need you. I am weak," he says. "You are strong."

"I don't think you are," I says. "I think you are a fine, good man."

"Thank you," he says, and we walked around the goddess and straight behind her was a wide road going down wide steps to the temple.

It was a wide, low temple that was set down the steps below us. It was made out of green and black stone and about as big as the Art Museum.

We come down that long wide flight of shallow steps and there didn't seem to be nobody anywhere. And finally we got down to the front door. It was open, and just as we got in front of it, I sure did jump.

There was the boom of a great big gong, and then something inside the church that sounded just like little ponies, a lot of 'em, galloping across a wooden floor. This noise stopped again, and then voices together like people praying.

As we got to the door, an old old man was standing in the shadow. He looked at the prince but he didn't look at me at all. We went in through a dark hall and then into a huge big church with no windows and no pews and no Stations of the Cross or anything to make you feel at home.

Well, it's no use trying to tell all about it, because if anybody's been to the movies enough you don't have to describe nothing much. They know what it looks like. And that's just what it did.

The prince went to a kind of altar and I followed him and it was the same lady like up the hill, but here she was littler, still with that small smile, and I didn't know what to do so I didn't do anything.

The prince kind of knelt down in front of her and kind of fell over at the same time, then he came back to me and we walked up two steps and sat on a stone seat with a back that went nearly up to the high dark ceiling. The gong went boom again and the ponies started galloping on the hardwood floor and stopped like before, and went on just the same and stopped again.

The old man brought a thing like a long candle but made out of wood painted blue, and the yellow flame turned blue as he set it down in a thing in the stone wall. Then he went and got some more of the same so we could see better right where we were. Then the old man went away and we sat on the stone seat and waited.

"He goes to get the wise men," says the prince, and he didn't say anything else till a door opened in the dark wall, and the old man and four more men in long robes with funny hats on came in.

The prince went down the steps and met 'em, and they spoke quietly. Each one touched the little lotus flower that the prince always wore, and then they said some more.

The door opened again and two little boys with bald heads led a man through it. And he come up and felt the lotus button, and when the light flickered on his face I saw that he wasn't just a blind man. I saw that his eyes had been burned right out. I heard the prince draw in his breath and ask a question, and they told him something. And then the two boys led the blind man out the door, and then the other wise men went out. And there was the big gong and the ponies again.

The prince gave a sigh.

"What happened to his eyes?" I says.

"My brother," he says. "The priest would not help him, and he had his men do things to the priest. You are right," he says. "When the English came to me," he says, "and asked me about my brother I could not tell them. But I went away to get more money than the Japanese will give my brother and keep him from doing these things. But for all my long trip I have not saved him. But in going away," he says, "I have found you. You are everything I want. You came here alone, American way," he says. "And so tomorrow, if they find my brother, I do as you say. Then I have you near me always."

"Tomorrow?" I says.

"Perhaps," he says. "If not tomorrow, the next day."

Before I could say anything the door opened and a man came in and spoke to him, and the prince went with the man through the door, and there I sat on that big stone seat all alone.

I sat for a long time and something came over me that took me back to a church in Springfield one night.

It was the last night, long after Willie was convicted, the very last night before what they had sentenced him to. And they sent word we could go to the Springfield prison to see him and we did.

A tired-looking priest went in with us and there Willie sat, clean-shaven and his hair cut. He hardly said a word, and we tried to think what to say. Suddenly Willie looked like a little boy again and, "Sis," he says, "I been bad, but I swear that girl wasn't my girl and honest I never meant to kill Dr. Harwood," and I had to believe him.

Later we went away, Pop and me, and we walked and walked, and when the light began to come, we knew it was nearly time for it to happen. Pop walked into a little Catholic church and blessed himself. I hadn't never seen him do it before. And we said our prayers, and there were some nuns praying up near the altar. And I sure was glad we went into that little Catholic church, though I would never have suggested it if Pop hadn't have just gone in.

And here it was just as quiet away over here, somewhere in India, and quiet voices of people praying to whatever they was worshipping.

Nobody seemed to be around so I just slid off of the stone seat and walked down the steps and over to the shrine and I blessed myself and knelt down and asked whoever the lady was in their religion to keep an eye on Pop till I could get back to do it myself. And I prayed and prayed.

Then something touched my arm, and there was the prince kneeling beside me. He and the priests must have come back, for there they were all around us. And I knew that when he had seen me kneeling there he must have thought this meant what it didn't mean at all, that I was ready to worship what he worshipped, so I got up but I remembered to bless myself.

"Listen, I said a little prayer to your virgin," I says, "that nothing bad will happen to you because I like you, and I said a prayer, too, that I will get home safe to my Pop that needs me and that I love. I don't guess," I says, "that she will mind. She looks so kind, even though I ain't her religion," I says, "and I guess I won't never be."

Neither one of us said anything for a long time.

A door opened and slammed shut, and a young priest came running across the floor like the wind. And as he came running he told 'em why he had come and they all ran for the door like the devil was after them.

Before I knew it, I was following 'em. Up the wide flat steps we all ran and I saw that out the other doors of the temple other priests were all running to the top of the steps at the back of the statue.

When they got to the top of the steps, they ran right around the statue, but I got to the top just in time to see the prince stop like an arrow had hit him. The priests stopped too, but I kept on till I could see what they saw.

Some Indian soldiers were bending over praying in front of the goddess, and right in front of her was a tall dark man with great black eyes. He had turned his head and looked at the prince, and now he got up slow and the soldiers behind him did the same.

It was the brother of Halla Bandah Rookh. And they had met on the same spot where they had cut their wrists and made their oath, and I saw in the brother's face that he was a hard man and a dangerous man.

The two brothers stood like that for a minute, and then the prince walked slowly towards the other one, and I saw the prince reach up and take off his little lotus flower button and all of a sudden I felt like I was seeing something I had no business seeing. So I edged around the priests and went to where I had seen the car. And I got in and shut the door, easy.

Through the jungle, I saw first a shaved head over a rock and then more and more till it seemed like from all directions hundreds of these priests were moving quiet as cats towards the statue.

I knew something awful was happening between those two brothers that had loved each other so and had sworn never to be against each other in anything but always together. But I just sat still in the car with my hands clasped and my eyes shut and I prayed for the prince to be saved from what I knew was coming to him if this didn't work out like I hoped.

Then the prince spoke pretty near right in my ear.

"Please," he says, "go to the house of my father. If I can, I will come. I beg of you do not tell a word of what you have seen here, not to anybody."

He looked pale and old and sick and tired, poor little Halla Bandah.

"I won't," I says. "I'm so sorry about it."

I knew somehow it was going to be to the death between those two, but I couldn't say anything more, because the two men that drove the car came from nowhere, and got in.

We drove off through the jungle by another road, so I didn't pass in front of the statue, and I was glad because I didn't want to see what I knew was going on there.

I had a lot of time for thinking about things, riding along through India by myself. But I just thought mostly about nothing and looked at the places we passed. Some of the people that we passed sure looked at the prince's car and me in it. And I thought maybe it was because I had on about the only woman's hat in India. That's what I thought, till I saw Lady Burroughs' hat.

"But surely," I thought when I met her, "the Indians

must be used to looking at everything Lady Burroughs wears." Because she had been in India twenty-seven years and I sure believed when I saw her that everything Lady Burroughs had on had already been seen by the Indians every year since she had been in India.

We went on driving towards the old prince's palace, and we got there all right, except for a truck that had some English soldiers standing around it because it was stuck in a ditch, and some Indians were helping 'em like I've seen farmers help with their mule to pull a car out of a ditch in Illinois. This was just like that exactly, except that these farmers had their skirts tucked up between their legs, and a whole sheet around their heads falling off on one side, and the mule was different, too, because over here it was a very big elephant.

It was a trick elephant, too, and strong and far tamer than any mule I ever saw. A lot tamer it was than those English soldiers crowding around our car.

I didn't know they were English because it seemed like the English I had met in Calcutta spoke like us, or anyway enough to understand pretty good. But as near as I could make out from these English their army was made up of some people that didn't speak English hardly at all. They are called Cockneys and these fellas didn't look like they'd ever been to a dentist in their lives and didn't even brush 'em.

I couldn't understand 'em hardly at all, but they could understand English. You see, I got tired of sitting there with them crowding all around and cutting monkey shines over me and my silk stockings and my white clothes and making remarks in the Cockney language and them laughing and not caring if the elephant never got their old truck from across the road. So I got a little mad and stuck my head out and I says, "Listen, big boys," I says, "this is all a lot of fun but if you bright boys don't take your eyes off of me for a minute and get a two-by-four and a rock to bend it on and ease that back axel up till Jumbo can get a hold on it, you're going to strain a mighty good elephant."

Well, sir, they sure looked surprised that I knew what to do in a case like that, and I guess it was funny, me all in white in that beautiful car with two men in uniforms driving me.

But they sure understood me, and they got a move on and did it just like I told 'em and it worked, and did that elephant give me a grateful look as we drove by. The Cockney boys all grinned with their snaggle teeth and gave three cheers as I waved to 'em and we drove away.

And that's how I learned what I didn't know before, that Cockneys are really Englishmen, and pretty fine Englishmen at that, as I learned from what Boggs did for Roddy and me. He saved our lives I guess by drowning himself and he did it like you wouldn't believe—smiling and making a joke.

The English are funny about a lot of things but when it came to scratch they sure were there for me.

So we kept on, till we got to where we was going to, and where we was going was something, I can tell you. Another movie palace but an A picture if I ever saw one.

All white it was, and covered with ruffles and borders of white stone lacework around the doors and windows.

And it was clean and pure looking, like the main building in Heaven.

I got out but nobody could speak English of any kind, so I couldn't tell the ones that opened the car and helped me out, or the ones at the main door of the house, who I was or what I was doing there. Come to think of it, I didn't know the name of who I had come to call on. But I guess I talked pretty loud trying to make 'em understand, so finally there was Aunt Mary and then everything was all right, because she could speak so many kinds of talk I called her Mrs. Berlitz. That's the name of a school that when Millie first saw Curly and thought he was a Spanish, she went to see about studying it. So she studied Berlitz, and look what it done for her.

Aunt Mary asked me about the prince, and I just said he had gotten delayed and we had better send the car back for him, and she did.

So we went into a big big room and that's where I met Lady Burroughs, and that's where I met her husband that I had heard about, I'll say.

He was a general and a sir, to boot, and I found out there was still another kind of an Englishman.

For Sir Gerald Burroughs wasn't silly at all, but was enough to scare you to death, barking like a Saint Bernard instead of talking. But he didn't mean it, as I found out later. And when I did, I couldn't help smiling, thinking of an old saying Pop used to say, "A barking dog will never bit." Then Pop would laugh and say, "Or maybe it's a barking dog is worth two at a bush."

Sirs and ladies are called a lot of different ways. For

an instance, Lady Burroughs was called that by me. She's "her ladyship" when the servants speak about her, and "my lady" when they speak right at her. And General Sir Gerald Burroughs, K.C.M.G., is just Sir Gerald to me and the servants and everybody, talking about or talking to. I asked Aunt Mary and Lady Burroughs together what the K.C.M.G. meant after his name.

Aunt Mary said it stood for Knight Commander of Michael and George, though I never found out who they were, and Lady Burroughs laughed like a horse and, "Not at all," she says. "When you know Gerald better you'll discover that K.C.M.G. stands for Kindly Call Me God."

I knew she was joking so I laughed, but I didn't always know when she was.

I wrote all this down in my book so as I would remember it, but I don't know why, as I don't ever expect to be able to use it, unless on Millie.

Well, I didn't see the old prince anywhere and I didn't like to ask, especially since Lady Burroughs ordered tea like it was her house. So we had it, too strong like always, but good things to eat with it and lots of 'em.

Lady Burroughs was called Agatha by Aunt Mary, and Sir Gerald she called just Gerald.

They called Aunt Mary just Mary.

Aunt Mary gave me some strawberries that were as big as my fist and cream so thick I thought it was ice cream but it wasn't.

I asked Aunt Mary if she had ever been here before and she said no, she had known Lady B. and Sir G. in England.

And Lady B. said Englishmen had to go home from India every so often or their livers got too appalling.

She said they were so glad to see Mary and to meet her charming niece because whenever they had seen her for years, she had always been telling them what a dear girl I was, and now they could see for themselves it was true.

This stumped me for a minute. Here was this English lady telling a lie and pretending to think I was what she must have known I wasn't. And old Sir Gerald agreeing too with his mouth full of toast and marmalade, though not talking, but just opening his big pale blue eyes and saying "Woof woof," which meant, "Yes, I remember it, too."

"Why would they do this?" I thought, especially with nobody in the big room for 'em to fool, but then I saw Mr. Bosco standing behind my chair, and I knew that this niece talk was for his benefit.

So I just ate the strawberries, like they did, by taking 'em by the stems that was left on 'em and swabbing 'em first in powdered sugar and then swabbing 'em in the thick cream and I knew I was among friends. Strawberries never give me a rash and I love 'em.

But I knew more than they did about Mr. Bosco, and he was a pretty hard little man to fool.

When the four men had taken the tea things away, Sir G. took Aunt Mary away down to the other end of the room, about half a square away, and Mr. Bosco and Lady B. and me sat down.

Lady B. smoked one cigarette right after another and talked about the war, and I was sure surprised at things she said about her own government. "Stupid, bungling British war office," she says, and, "Damned old British fuddy-duddies at Singapore that are so busy singing

Brittania Rules the Wave, they never think of looking up to ask who rules the sky."

She cussed and swore, all the time lighting one cigarette from the other and swearing worse than Millie when Curly left her.

So I thought she was maybe against her own country and for the Japanese, but I was pretty ignorant about the English then.

I didn't really understand 'em till we was on that rubber boat for so long, and me getting cooked in the sun like a piece of veal. It was then that I asked Sir Rodney Carmichael about it, and he did the same thing, talking about the government like that. It seems that all the English do it, and they go right on doing it all the time, and die like heros to keep anybody from changing the very things they have spent their lives cussing at, and that's England. Roddy tried to explain it, but I still can't quite understand it.

Lady B. had on an old black georgette dress, long but not the same length all around. It had a pattern of pink tulips on it and a pink satin girdle and two pink bows on the sleeves. It had been cleaned pretty often, but not often enough, so it was pretty limp. Her gray hair had never been done, it was just twisted up. Her shoes were gray kid oxfords with flat heels and her skin was like a piece of leather with brown spots on it. She had too many teeth and they were long and pretty crooked. She had a lot of gums too but her eyes was as bright and pretty as they had ever been. And somehow even with all of this she looked like a queen, and wasn't scared of the devil.

"You Burmese are going to be the crux of the whole thing in the East," she says, looking down at Mr. Bosco.

"Granted," says Mr. Bosco, "but fortunate for you, some of us are very loyal to your side."

"I hope so," says Lady B. and that was that.

Sir Gerald barked at Mr. Bosco to go and find out what time dinner was as if he was Simon Lagree in a play we gave at school. But Mr. Bosco didn't get mad like he might of, seeing as he was as rich as Rockefeller; he just got up and went to find out.

"Well," says Lady Burroughs, "you are an extraordinarily beautiful child."

"Thank you," I says.

"I thought all American girls were apainted, like our own," she says. "Why is your face so clean like a peach?"

"I wash it," I says, and she laughed.

"Listen," she says, "how much do you know about all of this business?"

"What business?" I says.

"This Indian business," she says. "Have you got any idea of marrying Halla Bandah?"

"No, ma'am," I says.

"Good," she says, "I was afraid you might have. He's rich and very powerful," she says, "but we aren't sure of him," she says. "That's why you are here, you know that."

I didn't know what to say so I kept quiet.

"You see," she says, "no matter how beautiful his eyes are, he'd still have to go to jail if he is arrested."

"He's really not like his brother," I says.

"That remains to be seen," she says. "Do you smoke?"

"No, ma'am," I says.

"Filthy habit," says Lady B. "Go over there and ask Sir Gerald to send me another packet of mine, and don't trip over that damned tiger's head on that rug."

When I got the cigarettes, Aunt Mary says, "I asked Lady Burroughs to explain some things to you." So I came back for more.

Lady B. didn't say "Thank you," but the way she said "Sit here," meant "Thank you," I guess.

"As I say," she began, "the old prince is all right, and we are reasonably sure of him. You see, he went to Oxford."

She didn't say when, and I didn't know where that was or whether he hadn't gotten back yet, but I didn't ask any questions.

"As I say," she says, "Halla Bandah is our problem. His brother is a stinker, a proper stinker," she says. "You see, their states being so near to Burma, they could be dangerous. So my husband, whose job it is know about such things, tried to get around Halla Bandah to find out their sympathies in all this business and he simply ran into a stone wall. Halla Bandah became a perfect clam. Before Gerald could learn anything, off went Halla Bandah to England. And Gerald found out that he was hoping to get a lot of money in your country, taking with him enough precious stones to sink a channel boat. And so your aunt Mary got the job of flying to America. Of course the prince didn't know he was being followed. Her job was to find out whether the money was to help the Japanese or not. Then he picked up the plane that our fat-headed intelligence didn't even know he had ordered, and then your Aunt Mary was troubled as he was about to get away from her altogether. But then this young American," says Lady B., meaning Mr. Wens, "thought up this fantastic scheme about you, so from then on your aunt Mary could not only follow him but travel with him. Is this all a great surprise to you?" she says.

"No," I says, "except that it seems like Aunt Mary is working for England in this. Is that right?"

"Yes," she says.

"What about Mr. Bosco?" I says.

"Who?" she says, and I told her I called him that.

"A good name for him," she says. "We don't quite know, but that little tea caddy knows quite a lot."

"He's nice," I says.

"Nice, yes," she says, "but nice to which side? We do know that Halla Bandah's brother is building an airfield, but whether Mr. Bosco is in on it, we are not sure. He's lived in Japan, did you know that?"

"He's all right," I says.

"Well," she says, "if Halla Bandah hasn't given us the slip he will be here at dinner, and when he comes don't be surprised if things pop."

"I won't," I says. "Do you think maybe he's run away?"

"Time will tell," says Lady B.

"I guess you work for the government," I says.

"My husband does," she says, "and though you'd never think it, he's very good at his job."

Mr. Bosco came back about then and said dinner will be at eight and that the old prince would ask to be excused from seeing all of them till then. But the old prince would like to see me right now in his room.

Well, believe me after what I went through with

those Soodans, I was scared to go, but Aunt Mary says, "Go," so I went.

Mr. Bosco took me along a narrow hall and up a set of stairs that I thought I was nearly to heaven when I got up it. And he opened the door and told me to go ahead, and I went on by myself through a gallery like, I mean it was a hall with one wall made out of stone lace that you could see out of.

It was getting dark and I felt like I was in jail.

I got to the end of it, and there was a door and it was a little bit open.

I waited a minute and then I just opened it and there was a big, big room with pretty near no window at all and just about as much furniture as there was window.

I couldn't see for a minute, and what I saw when I got so I could, I will surely never forget until I am too old to remember anything and that will be when I am dead.

I believe Pop was right about me having a good memory, but I didn't trust too much to it. Like Aunt Mary, I would write down if people said words that I wasn't use to and might forget, and that's how I remember now.

But I don't think I would have ever forgotten the prince's old father.

He looked just like God—not the Old Testament God, full of fire and war and eyes for eyes and teeth for teeth— he had a face that was old, but without a cross or a mean or a worried line in it. And gray hair in a long bob and a beard and a gray gown with some white and black on it, and he came towards me and I sure felt like crossing myself when I looked up into that beautiful face.

He smiled and held out both of his hands, and his hands were firm and warm. After we had looked at each other for a while, he spoke to me in a kind of English I had never heard, but it was the best English there is, you could feel that.

"I'm glad to see you," he says, "so glad." And we went to the only two chairs in the room, facing toward a dark wall, and we sat down.

"You are a Catholic, aren't you?" he says.

"Yes, sir," I says.

"Do you know Saint Cecilia?" he says.

"I've seen her pictures," I says, "playing the organ, with little angels dropping roses on her hands."

"I always thought that wasn't much of a blessing," he says, "having to play the organ with a lot of roses to get in the way of your fingers. Well, I think you look like Saint Cecilia."

"And I was thinking," I says, "that you look like God."

"Thank you," he says.

"Oh, that's all right," I says, "but you do."

"My son is in love with you," he says. "He wants to have you for his wife."

"Don't you worry about that," I says.

"I'm not worried," he says. "I only wish it was possible, but I know it is not," he says.

"You mean because I'm a Catholic?" I says.

"No," he says, "I mean because you are not in love with him."

"How do you know?" I says.

"Your friend Mr. Bosco told me," he says, and he smiled and so did I.

"He tried to get me to," I says. "Did he tell you that, too?"

"Yes," he says, "he did. But now he knows you won't do it."

"I couldn't," I says, "but I feel sorry for him."

"So do I," he says.

"Do you know what is happening at that cathedral, where I left him?" I says.

"Yes, I do," he says.

"Please tell me, is he safe?"

"What is safety?" he says. "In this world it is one thing we should not seek. Being safe is not as important as being right, and if we die for what we know to be right, is it not better than living for what we know to be safe?"

So we sat there quiet for awhile. And soon a little door opened, and two shave-headed priests came in with little tiny lanterns and then two more and two more, till there were quite a lot. From the light of the lanterns I could see that at the back of this arch was a kind of an altar. There seemed to be things, hooks like, or little brackets in the wall on each side of it, and they hung their little lanterns on both sides. And the light got bright enough for me to see that the altar was just two gold doors.

"That," he says, "is a shrine."

"I see," I says.

"There once was a great statue on a hill before this house," he says, "and there came an earthquake, many years ago, and the statue fell down and was broken to bits."

"I know," I says, "and the stone hand fell and rolled down the hill in the front door, with the ring on it, and so this house was blessed, and that's why you put the ring around your boy's neck like a holy medal. And the stone in the ring is called Hankah."

"And when Hankah was lost," he says, "you know who risked her life to get it back. But who told you the story of Hankah?"

"A Mr. Swift," I says, "in Chicago, that I always call Mr. Wens, like I call Mr. Bosco, Mr. Bosco."

"Is Mr. Swift a butcher?" he says.

"No, sir," I says, and I sure was surprised how much he knew about American history. "He's an FBI man."

"Oh, yes," was all he said. And we didn't say anything more till all the priests had gone out, two by two.

"Well," he says, "the wise men have come to bring Hankah back here, and I thought, since it was you that saved it for us, you might like to be here when it came home safe to rest," he says.

There was a clacking now, like the galloping of ponies that I had heard back there in the cathedral, only here they seemed to be mighty little ponies.

"What is that?" I couldn't help asking.

"Prayer wheels," he says, but I still didn't know what that meant.

The door on each side of the arch opened, and four of the same wise men come in, two at each door. And two of the wise men had a little pillar and on it was my old friend the big ring.

We stood up and the gold doors swung open. There, in a bluish light, was the big stone hand broken off at the wrist.

They said prayers and the old prince bowed over three times and I did, too. And the blind wise man came in, led by the two little boys, and he took the ring and held it up and red and blue lights shot out of it. While a soft, deep gong kept sounding he put the ring on the stone finger of the hand.

The men shut the doors and went out, and the priests took the little lantern down and walked out two by two, and the ponies galloped for a second, and the gong went, and that was all.

The old prince turned and took my face in his hands and he kissed me on the forehead, like I was being blessed by the bishop.

Then the other door away down where I had come in opened, and Mr. Bosco came in and took me away to the outside of what I guessed was my room. I guessed, too, that we weren't going to dress for this dinner. I hadn't brought anything as I didn't know how long we were coming here for.

But I didn't know *what* we had come here for, either, or I would have been more nervous than I was. So I waited for Mr. Bosco to say what he looked like he wanted to say, and when he said it I was sure surprised.

"You want to go home now. You finish your work, so, after tonight, you can go."

"You mean it?" I couldn't hardly keep from crying.

"I will miss you," he says. "What will you want to take with you?" he says.

"I don't know," I says.

"I have a present," he says, and he went away down the hall.

So I went in, and there was Aunt Mary combing her white hair and Lady Burroughs talking and smoking her cigarettes, and there was my best formal and slippers and lingerie and everything all laid out, and two girls to help dress with marks on their foreheads and all wrapped up in loose things like scarfs.

So we were ready to dress, so Lady Burroughs left us to do it, and I guessed she was going to, too.

I looked nice all in white, Aunt Mary said, and she wore everything deep blue. When we were ready we sat down until we were called to come and eat. While we were waiting I found out I was going to go home alone, by myself.

It seemed that Aunt Mary had to go to England, where she said she was with the intelligence, which I didn't understand, but that's what she said because I wrote it down, and that book I wrote it in was one of the three things the Lord didn't mean me to get home without.

Well, it was time and we went down.

We all met in another great big room with tapers like they light candles with in church, thousands of 'em, all around the walls. And there was Mr. Bosco in his same little suit, but everybody else, you bet, done up like for Cinderella's ball. Sir Gerald had his uniform on, instead of the old hunting coat and the wrinkled pants he had worn before. And he sure had a good corset to hold his belly in, and it did, too.

He had colored ribbons with teeny weeny little medals all over one side of his bosom, and his hair brushed straight up on the sides and his mustache straightened out real nice.

And there was Lady Burroughs, not looking like a rummage sale like she had in the afternoon. She was

thinner, too, in her corset and a black velvet formal and
rhinestones in her hair in a little crown like—or maybe
they were—diamonds—and a cigarette holder to match.
Aunt Mary and me were dressed like I said.

The doors opened and two soldiers came in wearing
uniforms and big striped things on their heads like
Franchot Tone and Gary Cooper in *Beau Geste*—that was
the first movie I can remember, but I sure never forgot it.

They got out of the way, and we waited and then the
old prince came in.

He was all in a fine quality white woven gown and a
long white coat thing to the floor. But the prince wasn't
there. And he didn't come and he didn't come. Finally
I guess the old prince knew we couldn't wait all night
so we went to the table and sat down.

I talked to Aunt Mary, like you do, with just my eyes,
indicating the place across the table that was set for
him but stayed empty.

Aunt Mary just shrugged her shoulders.

So we ate, and it was good. Each of us had a man to
take care of feeding us, but the man to serve the prince
had nothing to do.

I felt like the old prince was taking his time with the
dinner. And after awhile we sort of ran down and couldn't
think of much to say, except Lady Burroughs, and everybody was glad, I could see, for her to go on and on.

The food was all served in a most civilized way, with
silver and gold dishes, but after awhile we couldn't just
go on forever and so we went into still another big room.
The room was on the ground floor and along one wall
of it were tall windows, round at the top with stone lace

over 'em and no glass. They opened right out into the black night. Lady B. went on talking.

At first I wasn't right sure, but I began to think I heard something, away off, a soft clattering and rattling and a jingling, like a lot of horses walking or foxtrotting over a gravel road.

Pretty soon they all heard it, and Lady Burroughs looked real relieved that she didn't have to keep on with her talk anymore. So she stopped.

From then on we just sat there and waited, except Mr. Bosco. He couldn't stand it and he got up and nodded to the old prince and walked straight out of the room towards the front doors.

By this time it was plain that the clatter and the jingle was being made by maybe a hundred horses out there in the dark. And we heard 'em ride right up to the house.

There was a sharp order and the horses stopped. Then there was another order, and the men all got off and chains jingled and horses blew their noses, and suddenly there was Mr. Bosco.

"Your son is here," he says.

The old prince got up, and we all got up, too.

"Which one will it be?" I thought.

Then we heard a firm quick step, in boots, coming along the stone floor of the hall and I thought to myself, "It's not Halla Bandah, in his little soft gold slippers. It's the other one," I thought.

Then he got to the door and came just one step in and stopped there with his heels making a pop of a sound, and I thought to myself, "It's nobody I ever saw before in my life."

But it was, you bet. But what a difference.

Halla Bandah looked tall, and no wonder. He was in a uniform just about like Gary and Franchot and with boots with heels, and with the things on his shoulders to lift them up. And with the big high thing on his head he was nearly as tall as Gary and that's taller than anybody.

He stood there like a soldier, and like a soldier he spoke to the only other one of us that was a soldier—General Sir Gerald stood and listened to him like on a battlefield.

"I came to report, sir," he says. "My soldiers are ready to go where we are sent," he says. "I went away to sell what I could, sir, to get money to buy my brother back to us so he would not make friends with the Japanese. Before I go, sir, I did not like to speak my fears about my brother, so when you asked me, I would not talk, even to my father. But, sir, before I can return, my brother took orders from the Japanese, and I found out that he was going to build an airfield like he would plant an orchard, so now I have come to tell you, sir, and to my father I must say that my oath with my brother was a bad oath, so it is no longer."

His eyes looked bigger than ever but he said the next thing he said slow and quiet.

"Sir," he says, "I have done what I think is my duty. I have taken over my brother's state, I will use the money I collected in America and Africa to finish the airfield for the British. And, sir, me and my soldiers," he says, "are now at your service." And he saluted like Nelson Eddy in *West Point*.

Then he walked over and kneeled before his father,

and he held up his two hands. In each one was a little lotus flower button. And the old prince put his hand on his boy's head and blessed him.

Everything was still for a minute. Then the old prince said, "Where is your brother now?"

The prince got up and said, "I have had him arrested in the name of my father."

The father stood still a long time, then he said, "You have done well." And he excused himself and took the prince away, and Aunt Mary let me cry all over her dark blue formal.

So we went upstairs and sat and talked with Lady Burroughs while Sir Gerald was with both princes, old and young, downstairs.

We talked it all over, but I didn't talk much, because I had seen the old prince's face and I knew how he felt. That old man was a saint if I ever saw one, and I loved him and I couldn't get out of my mind the prince in his uniform, kneeling before that old man. And that hand of the old man that was about the color of the stained white keys that had turned brown on Aunt Helga's square piano—I'd never heard her play it till that one night right after Uncle Ulrich's funeral.

So the next morning, we had breakfast in our room, and who should bring it up but Bill and Coo. There were flowers on the tray, same as always, a white orchid for me and something dark red that I had never seen before for Aunt Mary.

While we were eating, Aunt Mary told me that we were to go back in the car to Calcutta with Sir Gerald and Lady Burroughs. She said that I had done a good

job and that it wasn't Mr. Hoover that had paid for my
clothes but the British government, but she couldn't tell
me before. So she told me now.

She had had all my things moved over here from the
prince's house and she said I was welcome to take with
me whatever I wanted to, but since I was going to be
flown to Australia by the R.A.F.—which stands for
British Flying Core—I could only take one bag, and she
had picked out the best things for me to take in it.

Then she showed me a jewelry case that was very
pretty that had been hers, and she said she wanted me
to have it as a present.

I says, "What will I need that for?"

And she says, "You'll have a few little trinkets unless
I am very much mistaken. Besides," she says, "if I had
only sixteen strings of real pearls and an emerald anklet
I wouldn't feel entirely unadorned," she says.

Then Aunt Mary gave me a big wad of English
money, which is just like toilet paper with black printing
on it, but she said it was money and I guess it was, but
I never got a chance to find out. Then she gave me my
passport. I didn't know I had one, but it seemed that Mr.
Wens had gotten it and brought it with him to Mexico
City that time, and she had kept it for me.

It had that Fort Worth newspaper picture on it, and I
felt pretty important with a jewelry box and a passport
with my picture on it.

So we got ready to go downstairs, and then Aunt
Mary said she sure wished she had me for a real niece,
and I said I sure wished I had her for a real aunt and no
lie, and we was downstairs and into the big room with

the tiger head to stumble over. She left me with Mr. Bosco, and said we'd meet at the car when I was ready.

Well, he took me up those long stone steps and then through the gallery to the door of the chapel with the hand altar where they kept Hankah.

And there the old prince was, with the morning sunlight from the one little window shining on his white hair.

He had a little carved ivory box with silver on it, and he said he wanted to give me something to take with me—it was the chain that Halla Bandah had worn on his neck with the ruby ring, Hankah, on it. The chain was beautiful with flat little gold links and every link with some writing on it, and he said it was like a rosary in my religion, and that each link was a prayer for my safety. Then he said he wanted me to have something to take the place of the ring that I had saved, and he began unlocking the little ivory box with a tiny key. And the key turned and the little ivory box came open.

It was a diamond, and I knew it was no rhinestone because they don't make 'em that big.

It was set in a band of gold with a little gold ring on it for that purpose so he threaded the chain in it, and let it hang down and it just trembled and sparkled like a dewdrop as big as a hazelnut.

I couldn't thank him, because I knew what it was worth—maybe not the Wrigley Building but the Annex to Marshall Field's, anyway—and I thought of how kind it was of him. And I started to try to say thank you, but something came over me and before I hardly knew it I dropped down on my knees, and he put his hand on my head and I said a quickie Hail Mary and got up, and he kissed me on the forehead.

Mr. Bosco was waiting for me outside the door.

"You got your present?" he says.

"Yes," I says and I showed it to him.

"Very pretty," he said and he weighed it in his hand.

"Yes," I says, "but most of all I love it because he gave it to me."

"That's right," he said, "but still, very heavy, and very heavy diamonds make very pretty diamonds."

"You're a bad one, Mr. Bosco," I says.

"Granted," he says, and we walked down a few steps and he stopped again.

"I have no present for you," he says, but he sure didn't look sad about it.

"Don't you worry," I says, "I've still got that little green bug you gave me for Christmas."

"That little bug will bring you much luck, and many grandchildren. That little bug is made of jade," he says.

"It's very nice," I says, "so you see I don't need any going-away present from you, because I couldn't never forget you, Mr. Bosco."

He looked at me with one eye squinted.

"No," he said. "I have no present for you now, but I do have something. You don't smoke pipe?" he says.

"No," I says, "do the girls in Burma smoke pipes?"

"Sometimes," he says, "but I don't have a pipe for a little girl. This pipe is an English pipe. This pipe is a man's pipe. This pipe is a present for American gentleman."

"Who?" I says.

"Pop," says Mr. Bosco and he laughed and took a polished wood box out of his pocket and gave it to me.

I couldn't hardly see how to open it but I did. Inside of it, on a purple silk cushion was a briar pipe that I knew Pop would die for. Because for somebody that had smoked nothing but corncob pipes all the years I've known him, he knows more about briar pipes than old Mr. Briar himself.

Well, there it was with a gold band around the stem and a gold band let into the bowl, and I saw some writing on the gold and I looked and it said "Pop" on it.

I tried to thank him for Pop, but I couldn't.

"I guess I'm going now," I says.

"You be careful," he says, "you have a young man in Chicago?"

"Yes," I says. "Anyway I hope he's in Chicago. If I don't pass him on the way. He's a soldier," I says.

"Good," he says, "you be careful." And then he gave me a card.

"You ever need me, you let me know," he says, and I knew he meant it. So we shook hands there on those steep steps, and then he took me to the door of a room at the bottom.

"You go in there," he says.

"What for?" I says.

"You'll see," he says, and he put his little old black hat down on his ears and that's the last I ever saw of Mr. Bosco, except his hat, and I did see that again just once.

So I knocked on the door and Bill opened it, and Bill and Coo looked at me with solemn faces.

When I was inside the little room they both bowed

till they nearly fell over, with their hands behind 'em. And finally, both at once, they brought their hands out from behind their backs, and each one had a white paper flower made out of something like tissue paper, and they gave 'em to me. Then they both turned around and ran out of the room.

I just stood there with those two poor mussed up paper flowers in my hand and fished out my handkerchief, and believe me, I was glad I didn't wear mascara.

So finally I took my handkerchief down from my eyes and raised my head up, and there was Prince Halla Bandah Rookh looking at me.

It looked like he couldn't say anything.

"Listen," I says, "I'm so sorry for you. About your brother," I says. "I know what that feels like," I says. "And another thing," I says, "I got to ask your pardon for what I did to you."

"What?" he says.

"Well," I says, "I knew, after awhile, that you liked me," I says, "but I couldn't very well go back after I started, and I felt guilty, because you see Aunt Mary, she's not my aunt at all."

"I know," he says.

"Yes," I says, "you know now, but you didn't know she was watching you."

"I did," he says. "I knew all the time."

"Then why did you let her?" I says.

"Because," and his eyes were soft and sad and beautiful, "because so long as they thought that they had fooled me, I could keep you with me," he says, and he touched my hand.

Well, I couldn't say a thing to that.

"You were right not to marry me," he says. "This is a time for a man to go to war. But always, always, I will remember you, and your beauty, and your goodness," he says, "and that across this world somewhere, I have a friend."

He took the paper flowers and the wooden pipe box and the ivory diamond-and-chain box out of my hands, and he put them on a table. Then he took a little gold box out of his pocket and he put it between my hands. Then he turned them till the back of one was up and he kissed it, then he turned them over and he kissed the back of the other one.

"Do not open this little box until you are at home," he says.

"All right," I says, "but won't you tell me what it is?"

"Only this," he says, "it will keep you and yours comfortable as long as you live. Promise not to open it."

"I promise," I says.

"I will not say goodbye," he says, "but may your god and my gods protect you always from harm."

CHAPTER THIRTEEN

SO I TOOK THE LITTLE GOLD BOX and my other presents and I went out to the car, and there was Sir Gerald and Lady Burroughs and Aunt Mary waiting, with two of those Cockney soldiers to drive us. And Lady B. had on her funny hat that was like John Alden's if Priscilla had sat on it.

"Where in the world did you get those dreadful flowers?" Lady B. said.

"They're not dreadful," I says, "they was made for me by two of my dearest friends," I says, "and I'd rather have them than the Wrigley Building," I says, "or that old Thread Needle Bank, or anything in England, not leaving out the king," I says.

"So sorry," she says, and we got in and drove away. I took a last look back at the old prince's palace and it sure was the real thing.

Suddenly, out of a window high up, I saw an arm and it was waving a little old black hat, and I waved and waved till the sight of that little hat was cut off by the big trees and stuff.

When we got to Calcutta, Aunt Mary bought me a

khaki colored suit and hat, and we had tea at the British place where the government was at. Suddenly Lady B.— who I had asked the pardon of for getting mad about the flowers and she had forgiven me—suddenly she looked around behind the high-backed chair where she was sitting and she poked there hard with her teaspoon. There was a yelp from somebody that was back there hiding.

And "Roddy," she says, "Roddy, you fiend, stop this ragging and come out at once and meet this sweet and amazing child." And out he came with his hair all mussed. He had on a uniform with wings on him and ribbons all smudged that needed cleaning.

"This is Captain Sir Rodney Carmichael, called Roddy, and as bad as they make 'em. Look at her, Roddy, you're to take her to Australia. Won't that be jolly? She's a Yankee?"

I wondered again why the English can't seem to forget the Civil War. They're always calling you that.

"How perfectly ripping," says Roddy and he gave my hand one shake and let go of my hand, but his eyes went all over me.

Sir Gerald cleared his throat and barked softly into his teacup. "And no tomfoolery, now, on the journey," he says.

"Last thought in my head, sir," says Roddy.

"And the first," says Lady B. "Yes, this bright little lad, as a reward of merit, gets the prize," and she patted him on the head and gave him a cup of tea.

Sir Gerald cleared his throat again. "Tell the truth, Roddy, is this a surprise?"

"Absolutely," says Roddy.

"You mean, you haven't been told by the old bear what you're to do?"

"Not a syllable," says Roddy with his little boy's eyes going around the curves of me, fit to skid into the ditch. "But I trust," he says, "it is not unconnected with international relations, lend lease and all that."

"It is indeed, she's a loan and not a lease."

They laughed a lot at that, but I sure thought it was too Eddie Cantor.

Then they talked about stuff I didn't understand. I can remember it, because I wrote it down. So here it is.

Lady B. says, "You are to take her tied up in Christmas ribbons and deliver her to old King Mark. You can look but you mustn't touch."

I knew they were joking, I mean English joking, but I didn't get it all.

And then Roddy says to me, "Are you fond of Tristan?"

And I said I never had any that I knew of. And everybody laughed and I knew I had made a mistake, but I didn't care much. I was going home.

So then Roddy got sent for and went with the soldier to the old bear's office to get his orders, they said.

Roddy was nice, if a little silly, like I said, acting full of stuff all the time when he talked to a girl, till he got alone with one all by himself, and then he stopped all of his foolishness and was just as nice as anybody. But I didn't know that then, and I was sure worried thinking I'd have to fly to Australia with this young fellow, all alone, just the two of us in some little plane. And if he was going to be so hell-bent on showing me what a boy he was, all the way, I didn't go for it much. But, as I say, all that was just for show. When it came to the point where he could have been a little troublesome—and it sure did, on that rubber raft—why he was pretty shy about it, and was I glad.

Of course I did have plenty of trouble with him later but that was after he got so full of fever. If it hadn't have been for his bad arm, Roddy, with his fever raging, would sure have been a hard boy to handle. And take it from one that's done it, a small rubber raft in the Indian Ocean is no place to fight for your honor.

Well, Roddy came back to the tea table and said it was all too absolutely something and the old bear had been "very red hot," whatever that meant. But anyway I found out what I had guessed already, that The Old Bear was the name they all called the head British council there.

But he wasn't an old bear at all, but a nice old boy that we had dinner with and stayed at his house.

The next morning at the first streak of day we got to the plane.

It wasn't a little plane at all. It was a big army plane, and had an English crew and guns, too, and was taking a whole raft of stuff, including me, to Australia and another passenger, too.

Just as we was about to start, Sir Gerald barked once, and then says, "You've got me to thank, Roddy, for this. They were thinking of giving her to the tigers."

Well, that sure gave me a start.

"But I wouldn't hear of it," he barked on. "No, I said this is a job for the British lion, I said, so I got the job for you."

Roddy laughed and says, "Don't let anyone know, sir, when we're taking off or those damned tigers may come dashing out of China and hijack her from me in mid-ocean—or is it hijohn? I forget."

I guessed they were joking about the tigers, but after that bloody lion and camels and elephants, I couldn't be just sure.

"Shut up, both of you," says Aunt Mary, laughing, "you'll scare the child to death." Then she turned to me. "The tigers, my dear," she says, "are the greatest American heroes of this war, to date. Colonel Chennault and those boys of his in China," she says, "are tops. And any girl that wouldn't jump at the chance to be hijacked—not johned, Roddy, my lad—by those boys," she says, "well, all I can say is, she doesn't deserve any such good luck."

"Very true, indeed," says Roddy, and we started saying goodbye.

"Well, cheerio, sir," says Roddy.

"Cheerio," says Sir Gerald.

"Cheerio, Lady Burroughs."

"Cheerio."

And then they all said cheerio two or three more times.

"Goodbye," says Aunt Mary, and we got in, and I says hello to all the boys, some Cockneys and some like Roddy, but all nice and making a few cracks, but nice, too.

Just before we started, a soldier ran up and gave something to Sir Gerald. He gave it to Aunt Mary, and she opened the envelope and there was another one inside of that one, and "Hey," she says, "you're always getting letters just before you take off."

"Me?" I says, and I couldn't breathe hardly.

"You," she says, and she gave it to Boggs—that was the sergeant with the wings. That looks funny when you write it, a sergeant with wings, but when I think of Boggs now—and I could never forget his funny crooked little face—a sergeant with wings is exactly the way to tell what he really was like.

I couldn't understand hardly a word Boggs said till I got to know him better, but that first morning, I sure loved him when he handed me that envelope that had come halfway around the world from I could guess who.

So I don't remember the goodbyes, or the takeoff or anything much, but that suddenly we were in the air and I was sitting quietly so my goose pimples would smoothe out before I opened my letter that was surely from Jeff.

Millie says to me once, "You're a funny one," she says. "Here I am always honing for Saint Louis where I was born at, and you just go along and home is wherever you hang your slip up."

Well, I did always try to act like it was, and I guess I made it seem like it was that way with me, even when it wasn't, because what's the use of squawking all the time.

But now I thought about Jeff, and how I hadn't really thought of him much, just that he was big and nice looking with a smiling kind of face—like a nice horse, but kind, that was what I first saw in Jeff. He had big feet and his beard grew fast—he was always smooth when he came to work every night, but by morning I could see a stubble, like the sun on a cut wheatfield, while we sat, having coffee together at the Greek's. And how I never thought much about him till that night, or maybe I did and didn't know I did. But anyway, I sure had thought a lot about the way his arms felt around me in the sunrise at the airport. And I knew all of a sudden that Jeff was what I wanted, that with Jeff everything I hadn't wanted with anybody else would be different and here I was, at last, headed for home. And a letter from Jeff in my hands, and what a fool I was to be sitting thinking when I might be reading it. So I opened it fast, and here it is, what I remember of it.

"For the love of Davy Crockett where are you at?" That's how it started.

That Swift feller seems to know, so I am sending this to him. I could ring his neck for knowing and me not knowing. I could if he hadn't gone to see your pop when he was so sick and got him into the hospital in Mattoon, and it ain't costing your pop a dime. Being as I am in this man's army, now, I can't go like I did before. I will try to see him before I leave Wednesday. Hope my last letter found you as it left me, well and so full of love and crazy about you, and thinking about you getting back soon, and about you and me.

I don't like to ask young Swift about you as he says things like: "never was such a girl," and like that. I never thought I was jealous, except for once of a man in Texas that my pony Rowdy would walk right off from me to follow. But I guess I was wrong about myself, so you better get used to the idea.

About you and me, I was all right until one morning about sunup, we were having a cup of

Java at the Greek's and I stood up over you and I smelled your hair, and it didn't smell like perfume, but like the puppy I was crazy about when I was a kid and I kept washing her all the time with the most expensive and pretty-smelling soap I could find. So then I knew my goose was cooked.

I will add a postscript onto this after I see Pop Wednesday or maybe Tuesday, as I don't know which at this writing, so I will stop now and say goodbye. But, oh, if I ever get you back again, I will sure hold on to you and smell that good clean smell of your hair, close, and it will be a damn good thing you don't wear lipstick to get smeared around all over both of our two faces, and I won't stop but just keep on forever and ever, amen.
Your friend and well-wisher,
Jefferson Davis Wade.

P.S. Wednesday. I couldn't see Pop but here's a letter he wrote and with it is one long kiss from me. Jeff

More P.S. Did I say I got orders? They say I got to go away—where I don't know till tomorrow, if then, and couldn't say if I did or do. But will keep in touch with Pop and he can tell you where I am at, if I know.

If it is China or Alaska or the Dutch Indies, I'll try to get Swift to stop you so you can stay there until I can get there, as you seem to get to every-

where. But wherever it is, I'll be loving you and
missing you always. Hoping you are the same.
Your friend and well-wisher,
Jeff

The letter from Pop smelled like his old corncob
pipe, and I had to read it slow, because I was getting to
be a crybaby and I couldn't see half of the time.

Dear Podner, Jeff was headed this way, but a
strong military wind blew him off of his course.
However Ted Swift says he will give this to Jeff
to send it with his letter, as he will see Jeff tonight.

Ted Swift gave me the money again that you sent,
but where you got so much I don't like to think,
because surely I didn't bring you up to rob banks.

Aunt Helga looked at your mystery-woman
pictures in the papers, and so did everybody else
who wasn't blind, and all she said was: "what is
it about our family that gets us always in the
papers?" And it sure is true.

I didn't mind, you looked prettier than Lillian
Russell to me, and that lady with you looks alright
for a chaperone.

I am alright now or soon will be, I hope, just
took on a job that was too stout for me, getting
gravel and filling in that low place in the south
corner that keeps washing in. I thought it was a
good idea, there's so little I can do for Aunt Helga.
But don't ever say anything even to me about it.
I thought by saying this to you I'd let you know I

knew, because we are and have always been podners, haven't we?

Don't you worry about anything as I am not worried about you. But if you ever get around to it you better take a good look at Jeff—or maybe you have.

So long,

Pop

PS. Got a letter around first of the year from the place up on the hill. It says your ma's just the same and a note on the bottom from Dr. Morrison says she seems contented.

Well, that gave me enough to think about all the way to Australia and back, if I had of rode the whole journey on a lame Kangaroo. But I had to stop thinking for awhile— or anyway to put it off till another time—for there was Sergeant Boggs saying, "Got some letters, huh?"

"From my Pop," I says.

"Everything all right?" he says.

"Sure," I says.

"You flown before?" he says.

"A little," I says.

"How much," he says, without the "h."

"Well," I says, "Chicago to Mexico City, to Rio, to Natal, to Liberia, to Khartoum, to India, and now this," I says.

"Gawd," he says.

"Why do you ask?" I says.

"I just wanted to know whether to bring you a cup of tea or a paper bag," he says.

"Tea," I says, and he brought it. So, after he took the cup away and before he could get back, another boy sidled in beside me. He was the other passenger to Australia. He had a uniform and wings and ribbons and a kind of a cowboy face.

"I'm Cecil Dillon," he says, and he was like a mixture of the kind of an Englishman that Roddy was and the kind of a Cockney that Boggs was, but better educated than one and maybe not quite as much as the other.

"Hello," I says.

"Got letters from home?"

"Yes," I says.

"I'm going to Sydney," he says.

"Who's that?" I says, and he laughed and told me that was the name of a town in Australia, only he called it just Strylia. He showed me what he called the wife and the kids, and they sure looked sweet. Cecil, the boy, took after him, and Nell, the girl, after her.

He had to pick up his family at his mother's place in another town (that I forgot as soon as he told me) where they were waiting for him, and they would all go back to Sydney for his leave.

He had been flying out of England over the channel for ten months now, and he said there wasn't much danger of any sort of a show on this jaunt we was taking. But he was jumpy, I guess it was from what he called channel-hopping, and kept on looking out of the plane, like something might be following us.

Cecil had long legs and big hands like Jeff. He said his father was in sheep, and showed me a picture of a lady that was called the mater, and she had three plumes in her hair and a very old-fashioned satin dress and long gloves. He said she had had to go to court and that the picture was taken before she came out, but I didn't like to ask what any of it meant. I was glad for him to talk because once he got started that's what it seemed like he had been busting to do.

After he talked I don't know how long, just suddenly in the middle of a word he was asleep and all the tightness and braveness had gone out of him. His head slid over onto my shoulder, and I kept real still so he could rest. And I'm so glad now I did, especially when I think of that little folder with the pictures floating on the water where I couldn't reach it with the piece of propeller.

So now at last I had a minute to think about Jeff's letter and Pop's.

I knew how slim my chances were of getting to the place Jeff was coming to. And Pop's letter—saying that he was in the hospital and was sick, which he had always been but must be worse now because he'd graveled-in the low place on the south side of Aunt Helga's yard.

I could see me and Willie sitting there when it was damp, like it always was there. Aunt Helga said it was nice because things grew in that spot that she couldn't get to grow anywhere else on the place. But I took Willie there to try and teach him about the toadstools that would pop up after a rain, that they were poison and he shouldn't touch them and then put his thumb in his mouth.

That was when he was little and we'd go to see Aunt Helga on Sunday before our house burned up. And Pop, what a one he was to know things, and me thinking I was the only one that knew it. But he must have known it all the time, or he would never have said that about filling it in with gravel to let me know he knew, and Aunt Helga saying our family was always in the paper and she sure was right.

I could see Aunt Helga now, at Uncle Ulrich's inquest, sitting there as placid as Saint Ann in the picture, answering questions. Then this city doctor asked if he could ask the widow a few questions.

And the coroner said, "Certainly I am sure the widow will not mind. Go ahead, doctor."

So then this young doctor, he asked all over again everything the coroner had asked. He would have heard it before if he hadn't been so late. He asked what they had for supper. Bean soup and coffee, whole wheat muffins, cabbage with vinegar, some of the beans strained out of the soup and the steak.

"That was all?"

"That was all."

"Was there butter with the bread?"

"Well, yes, I forgot that."

"Any preserves?"

"They was there, but nobody ate any."

"Any sauces for the steak?"

"No, sir, he never liked those bottled sauces."

"Any pickles?"

"No, sir, I hadn't opened any."

"Just the steak, plain."

"Just the steak, plain, with the mushrooms."

At that the doctor sat up in his chair. He wanted to know how the sauce was made. But it wasn't exactly a sauce. It was more like just mushrooms, fried in butter in a pan.

No, Uncle Ulrich never liked to carve, he got so tired cutting meat in the shop, so she always put it on the plates in the kitchen and brought it in.

He wanted to know where she had gotten the mushrooms.

She said Uncle Ulrich had brought them home with the steak.

That would do, ma'am, he said, and he thanked her very much.

So then we all had a cup of coffee and waited for the verdict. It came back accidental poisoning, and we all got apologized to. They said it couldn't have been helped, because there must have been a bad mushroom or maybe a toadstool on the steak. But whatever it was, it must have been just one and it got onto Uncle Ulrich's plate, and that's why nobody else had been poisoned to death like Uncle Ulrich had. And it was sure a regrettable tragedy, him just about to become an alderman, and they were sure sorry to disturb a lady at such a time, but the funeral could be the next day and we had their deepest sympathy.

Aunt Helga was right, our family does get in the papers, but sometimes we don't when we might, and those are the times when it's a darn good thing we don't, and that time was sure one of 'em.

Roddy got relieved from his piloting and came and sat with me, after Cecil woke up.

Roddy acted a little smartalecky again, but nice too, and funny, talking like I had learned to expect from his kind of English by referring to big things as if they were little, calling Lady B. The Perfect Picture of the British Unicorn, which I sure had to write down not to forget it. He said this was a picnic that he had taken a few times but never with such dainty supplies.

The others heard this, like he meant them to, so they called out jokes about him not overstaying his leave from the controls while he was inspecting the cargo. But they were nice, and we all had sandwiches that were sure good. By now there was nothing to see but sky up there and water down there and us. And then for a long time just clouds and no sky and no ocean—just us.

So we stopped at places and I got so I could understand Cockney just like a native, except when it was too Cockney. But I'd say, "Hey, Boggs, remember I ain't educated in English," and he'd laugh and talk slow like to an idiot. And it was like a game, whether I could or couldn't understand.

He said Cockneys are called Tommies—all of 'em that are not N.C.O.'s, I didn't know what that meant, but didn't want to be always asking him.

Wherever we stopped was English, at least there were a lot of Tommies, and did they open their eyes when a regular big army plane came down and landed and then I stepped out of it. I was glad I was dressed in the same color as them. So they thought at first that it was a uniform, but when they found out it wasn't, they thought I was what they called a Musical Gel and they wanted me to sing or dance.

Roddy was a wonderful boy. He tended to everything. He was friendly with the men, as he called 'em, and was what the English call cheeky to the senior officers and red hats.

Singapore was a fort, like on an island, and absolutely safe so they didn't have to worry about the war.

So I told Roddy what Lady B. had said that day to Mr. Bosco about Singapore singing about the wave and forgetting about the sky. And he looked at me hard, and "Don't tell that to these red hats," he says, "or we'll get court martialled." Then he drank his Scotch, which he could sure store away and never fall down flat. And he grinned, slow, and he says, "That old tea cosy," meaning Lady B., "knows nearly as much about British weakness, my pet, as the Japanese army does."

And he gulped down the last drop, and we went out and climbed in, and off we went.

The equator is not like they taught us it was at all. I remember my teacher saying "The equator is an imaginary line around the center of the earth that divides the northern hemisphere from the southern hemisphere."

Well, that's a lie. For I looked and we all looked when we crossed it and no imaginary line could any of us see, even with opera glasses.

I liked Boggs, he was my friend. He had lost everybody he'd ever had, his wife and his father and three kids—all except one brother that was in prison when the Germans laid eggs on the East End, as he called London. When he found out I had a brother that had been like his, he quit thinking I was a society toff, as he called 'em, and we was good friends, and I won't never forget him. And certainly I won't never forget that stocky little man standing there on one leg on the top of that wing of our plane that was sinking fast and looking back at Roddy and me through the fog. Roddy, far gone as he was, guessed what Boggs was going to do, and yelled all the English cuss words for him to please come back and let us all take our chances together.

But Boggs looked at us and grinned, and "Ow far is it to Margate?" he called, and stepped off of the wing into the water. He came up and waved his hand once and then swam out, rising up on top of a wave as big as an Indiana hill and going over behind it, till we couldn't see him for a long time. Then I saw him up on top of another. I yelled at him to come back but Roddy quit yelling because he saw it was no use. I saw him once more, and I knew he couldn't go on with his leg shot full of bullets like it was. And then I didn't see him anymore, and that was all. Just Roddy and me in the fog, watching the plane sink.

I guess I've got to tell about it, as near how it happened as I can. But I can't remember except little bits. We were flying in a fog and I was writing the English words that I wanted to remember in my book. Suddenly somebody yelled, and there was a roar right on us nearly, and something going pop, pop, pop, pop.

I looked and there was a flash of flame like a burning house falling through the sky and nearly going to hit us, and something out of it spitting more fire. And Boggs yelled. "That's it, mates, I got it."

And before I could say, "What?" Cecil lay flat on the floor, facedown like a train had run over him. All the time that streak of burning fire kept coming at us a mile

a minute and shooting past the windows as we bumped
and started going over sideways.

By then I seemed to know that the thing burning and
falling out there was another plane on fire, but it was
shooting the hell out of us as it went down. We heard it
hit the water, and boom, one big flash of light.

About that time we hit, and everything got all mixed
up together. I remember Roddy climbing back to me as
I searched through my bag to save something, and I was
so relieved when I found it. And then I don't remember
anything till I was in the water just coming to myself
and Roddy pulling the last of me into that little rubber
boat.

He told me afterwards that the bigger boat got sunk
with the plane. Just the tip of the wing was above the
water now, and it was just before this that Boggs had
done like I said, and was in the water, and Roddy
yelling, "You bloody, bloody fool, come back here."
And he sure was right, I never saw so much blood as
was on Boggs. But Boggs wouldn't come back, because
it was just the little boat, instead of the big one.

The wing tip disappeared and I saw Roddy's arm, all
bloody and hanging wrong. It was just us in that little
rubber boat with some stuff floating around us. I used
the piece of propeller and tried to reach that little leather
folder with Cecil's Australian kids floating away in it.

Then I tore strips off my skirt until I was nearly naked
to twist a tourniquet around Roddy's arm. It made Roddy
faint with how it hurt him, but it sure stopped the spurts
of blood just like that Scout master told Willie it would.

So there I sat, sort of laid down with Roddy in my

lap pretty near, and before I knew it, it was dark, and was I ever seasick. And days of two people together like what we were, delirious and sun-blistered and talking, gets you to be good friends or bad enemies or first one and then the other till you get rescued or die of exposure or anyway of embarrassment.

It wasn't till we had nearly got to Australia that we were picked up by the destroyer. The commander told me what had happened so I could tell Roddy when he came in to see me in the cabin that was turned into a hospital just for me. I had a sailor to look after me, though I could hardly understand him at all because he spoke nothing but Scotch. But all of the officers and most of the men came in to do anything they could.

I'm Swedish, see? All pale, like a white pidgeon as Millie use to say. And people that are Swedish are all pale like that. And people as pale as me learn early not to get sunburned, because it's just burn, blister, peal and heal, and then burn again worse the next day.

With no clothes on that Swedish skin and salt water spraying on top of it as it cracks, my skin turned white and dropped off leaving what looked like raw lamb underneath. That tan just about ruined me.

That's why when we got rescued I had to remember to try to think I saw somebody else entirely while the poor Scotch sailor that had a red cross on him greased me and bandaged me like a newborn baby. And the only reason I didn't blush was that I was worse than that color pretty near all over, not having had anything on worth mentioning all that time in that boiling sun.

So, while he was fixing me, the only thing that saved me from dying of thinking what was being done to me and by who, was that I pretended I was unconscious. Now here I was wrapped in clean white bandages all over me, except the very middle and the brassiere part.

What the commander told me was that the Tigers got in a dog fight, high up. They came out of China, those Tigers, just to get in dog fights, and that meant not what it sounded like, but shooting Japanese planes when they could find 'em.

Well, they'd found one that day and they'd chased him out over the water high in the air. So finally they shot him up bad and he slid off sideways with puffs of fire shooting out of him, here and there, into the fog that was below them. So the Tigers went home.

Well, when the Tigers got back they heard about what happened to us. It was news, I guess, because it seems that we weren't supposed to be shot at much, being just to carry stuff. And because of the fog the commander and the Tigers just had to guess what really did happen.

Well, they guessed that this Japanese plane, coming down through the fog with his tail burning, pretty near hit us, and the commander said he guessed the pilot must have decided to pop a few into us as he went down.

I had saved my book, because I had been writing in it when it happened. And even if it hurt my arm to write now, and even if the book looked funny after being dried out by Scottie, I didn't want to forget anything, since most of the girls I have met don't ever get to have things happen to them like what happened to me. But my grandfather used to tell me about the Civil War, and

I sure thought he was lying, but if he'd have had a book that he had wrote it all down in, I might have believed a lot more than what I did believe.

And, "Who knows," I thought, "I might get to be a grandmother someday, if all of me don't come off with these bandages, and I want to have something to tell my grandchildren and prove it ain't a lie."

The reason I thought about getting to be a grandmother was that one thing I had saved was Mr. Bosco's Christmas present, that little green bug that helps you get grandchildren. I had it around my neck on the chain the old prince gave me, but the diamond was in my bag with the other stuff.

That stuff about the grandchildren got me thinking about Jeff. I knew that if it was a movie, it would have been Jeff on his way to the war that first spotted our little rubber boat after all of those blistering days, and Jeff would have been the one to bandage and take care of me. Only I was sure glad it wasn't him, because if it had been Jeff instead of that Scottie, I wouldn't have just pretended I was dead, I would have been really dead, or anyway hoped I was.

But it wasn't a movie, so it wasn't Jeff that spotted me, or bandaged me, either.

Well, like Pop said, I sure get bunged up easy, but I sure get better in a hurry, too. I use to wish I could get tanned like Martine McCullough and the Gianini girls on Fredrica Street use to in the summer at the camp that I always wished I could go to that they went to. And if they called me Paleface when they got back, they sure should have seen me when I got to Australia, in a white English sailor suit and me as brown as an Indian.

Well, like I said, the commander thought I had better not turn his destroyer into a young ladies seminary. So I tucked my hair up inside one of the English navy caps. They're not flat on the top of your head, like ours are, but have a nice space for a girl's hair.

Well, there I stood on the bridge, as they called it. It was like the upper front porch of the boat, though they didn't like me calling it a boat, I was supposed to call it a ship. And there I stood with Roddy with his arm in a sling and the officers with us to see us come in to Australia, and I guess from the shore—even through opera glasses—I looked like any other sunburned sailor, but taller than the English ones.

Well, Australia sure looked good to me. The sailor that was on duty up on the bridge kept laughing and blinking a light slow and fast. Roddy said he was telling the shore man about us, and especially about me. He must have made it quite a story, for when we finally got in, there was a lot of fuss, with people and pictures.

The commander agreed with me that I had better not try to go through the town in that sailor suit, so somebody—a very nice girl named Rosalie—came to find out the sizes of everything, and when I was dressed I came out on the deck to say goodbye to all the boys. The commander had 'em all drawn up at attention but it looked too much like they had looked that day when they said a burial service for Boggs and Cecil and our other boys that didn't get saved. So I told the commander to go ahead and loosen 'em up so I could tell 'em goodbye. He looked a little shocked, but he did like I asked him. So then it was easier.

So, to my surprise, I talked a long time, about how brave an Englishman could be when he came up to scratch. And they thought I meant something about an old joke they've got about throwing a sailor in the ocean because he's got fleas, so they died laughing at me saying a sailor come up to scratch. So I acted like that was what I meant, but I got 'em to listen when I talked about how I wished I could tell their folks how good they had been to me.

How can you thank a lot of men like that for treating you like they done me? You can't, so I didn't try. But my eye lighted on that bowlegged Scotch angel that had taken care of me, and I just walked over and kissed him. You never saw a man turn so red, and you never heard such a yell from the others.

CHAPTER FOURTEEN

THAT NIGHT THE OFFICERS and Roddy all came to the American government's place for a big dinner, and they all brought newspapers about me and the rescue at sea of me and Roddy. And was it wonderful to meet some people that spoke American.

Of course, I didn't have any money, or my passport or just about anything at all, only my dried-out little writing book and what I had saved out of my bag when I dived into it just as we hit the water.

I guess something takes care of you times like that. I saved the paper flowers from Bill and Coo. They were soon melted and torn and just disappeared and I used the wire stems to twist around my hair to keep it out of my eyes. Then I had my little green bug that Mr. Bosco had given me, still on its chain around my neck. I'd also saved that little box I got in India. Something sure helped me and I saved that box. So when the time came I could open it—and I did, but that was a lot later, of course.

Well, after dinner, Roddy and me were standing on a balcony, like Jeanette McDonald and Nelson Eddy, and he was pretty, sweet and not smartalecky. He wasn't even very British, just sweet.

He said to make it all just like an adventure yarn, we ought to get married.

And I joked, too, and I says, "Yes, Roddy, can't you just see me going back to England as Lady Carmichael?"

And Roddy says, "Yes, I can." And I saw, for the first time, that he meant it. And was I surprised.

But it was sure a compliment, because I had learned a lot about Roddy on the destroyer—not from him, you bet, but from other officers. Those straight little stripes on his sleeve wasn't like he told me—to prove he use to be a sergeant—but they were wound stripes that Roddy got in other parts of the war. And his family was real stuff, and I sure felt obliged to him, even in the craziness of a war, to ask me that, and I told him so.

I tried to make him understand why it sure would be asking for trouble. Then I told him goodbye, and he was going to go very formal on me for not being fool enough to marry a gent like him.

But I says, "Listen, big boy," I says, "any two people that have been together for as long as us and has got things to remember like us—I mean about Boggs and Cecil and those other poor boys—that puts us pretty close together, for now and for always. So you snap to attention, Roddy, and march yourself over here and kiss me goodbye, or I'll tell whoever does get to be Lady Carmichael what a heller you are with a fever."

Roddy was a nice boy and he did as he was told. So we went back in and they all said they could see us plain on the balcony, like those black cutouts against the sky, and the upshot of it was I had to do a lot of kissing goodbye before they all left. But they sure had been nice to me, and I felt like they wasn't foreigners at all.

At the party were two American United States officers named Herb Furse and Jimmy Talbott. They were the ones that would fly me back with my new passport. And nice as the English was, was I glad I was going from here on home with American boys.

Mr. Warburton, one of the members of the American council, asked if he do anything for me before I left. I said yes, if there was any way to find Cecil Dillon's wife I wanted to see her. I said his mother must be a Mrs. Dillon, and she must live somewhere close and the wife and kids were with her waiting for him to take 'em home. Anyway, I told him they were in Australia, and from what little I ever saw of my geography, Australia was just an island, and so even if Mrs. Dillon was on the other side of Australia, maybe I could just run over and see 'em for a minute before I left.

He looked funny, but he called up two or three places, and after we waited awhile, it turned out Mrs. Dillon, Cecil's mother, lived right there where we was at, in this town named Melbourne.

He sent me in his car. He said he'd go with me, but I said I'd rather be by myself. So a soldier drove me, named Captain Breckenridge from the state of Virginia.

We got to a little house, and there were the kids outside. Little Cecil playing with a homemade airplane, and little Nell sitting on the steps watching.

They saw me and I got out and asked Breckenridge to wait for me.

Mrs. Dillon, the mother, came to the door and I asked her if Nell was home. She was in the dining room laying the table for some American soldiers they had invited to Sunday dinner—it was the first time in awhile I knew what day it was. She asked if I could stay, too, with the American boys that would be coming soon, but I said I was sure sorry, but I had an engagement with two other Americans that afternoon to fly across the Pacific Ocean.

They laughed and were very polite about it. And they invited me to please step in and rest my hat. I couldn't wait any longer, knowing what a shock it was going to be, so I told 'em who I was and why I had come.

They said, yes, they knew who I was the first minute I drove up. They had recognized me from the paper. They said they had had word from the Air Ministry. Preachers, I guess, for the flyers. They were kind and sweet, and showed me pictures of Cecil as a sheep herder when he was growing up.

So I told 'em about our trip together and how he loved 'em all, and that nearly the last thing he talked about was them, and for the first time since it happened I cried, and they comforted me like I had come to comfort them. And they never cried a tear.

I couldn't help saying, "Did you know all this, when you invited these Americans to come to this Sunday dinner?"

They said they had a few Americans every Sunday and they didn't like to disappoint boys so far from home, so they decided not to change.

Soon I had to go, so I told 'em goodbye and got in the car. Nell stood in the door and smiled at me. I waved and she waved, and we drove away, and Breckenridge agreed with me that they sure have got what it takes.

Being all Americans, Jimmy and Herbie and I had a lot of fun. I told 'em quick about Jeff, and I sure was surprised to hear myself say Jeff was my fiancé, and besides that, that we was engaged, which we certainly was not. But saying it like that made me feel good.

By the time we got to Hawaii I felt we were nearly home, and it made me think of going back to Mattoon that time. First, I got the telegram that Uncle Ulrich was dead when he hadn't been sick or anything. I got Millie to come back and squeeze into Butch's white satin formal so I could go, on account of Aunt Helga always being nice to me.

So I went, not knowing there was going to be any inquest, but there was. I was just going because I was so sorry for Aunt Helga, and I never thought anything strange had happened for a single minute. Until that city doctor asked again just exactly what they had for dinner. I still wasn't sure what was going on because Pop wasn't saying anything, but I had a strange feeling.

Then the inquest was over and we went home, and all Aunt Helga talked about was how Spot died of old age on Saint Patrick's Day and other current events.

I sat up all night, which is customary for me when I get to worrying. And I kept telling myself I was just imagining things. But I remembered watching Aunt Helga making coffee when we got home, quiet and gentle, with that little tight look around her mouth not so tight anymore. And me on through the night thinking even if she did, why would she do it now, after all this time?

The next day was the funeral, and the Lodge Brothers with their little aprons and badges had crossed spears to walk under. And there were speeches at Mr. Hawthorne's Undertaking Parlors and Chapel, and then more speeches at the grave.

We came home after that, inviting the aldermen and the mayor in for a drink of Rhine wine or beer.

The mayor took me aside and wouldn't let go of my hand while he was sympathizing with me. He said, "You're working in Chicago, I hear. Well, I get up to the city once in a while, we ought to get together sometime. How about it, little lady?"

Then it was just Pop and Aunt Helga and me having supper. The parlor was still open from the company, so we sat in there, though we never use to. Pop didn't smoke his corncob, because Uncle Ulrich never had liked it, but after awhile Pop, not thinking what he was doing, filled his pipe and tamped it down. Just as he was about to put the stem in his mouth, he saw what he was about to do and eased his old corncob back in his pocket.

Aunt Helga got up and walked out of the room, then we heard her coming back. She walked in and put a handful of big birdseye kitchen matches right on top of the velvet album that was on the table right alongside of Pop.

She took one, struck it on her shoe and held it out to Pop. He took out his pipe and she lit it for him and he puffed away.

Suddenly Aunt Helga turned and walked across the room with her cameo earrings swinging, and, bang, she opened the big square piano like a gun going off. And she sat down and stretched her arms out to get her wrists out of her sleeves, and bang, both hands down on those old yellow keys, her foot on the loud pedal. And for the first time I heard Aunt Helga play.

It was like a march, and I imagined soldiers and a circus and a carnival. She played it loud and hard, making my blood tingle. Then she got up and came over and kissed me.

"Let's go to bed and all get a good night's sleep," she said. And we did.

So now, nearly to Hawaii, I was kind of tingling with being so near home. I guess Hawaii ain't so near really, but it sure was nearer to home than India.

Anyway I was getting there, and Herbie said I could send a telegram from San Francisco where I was going to, right after Hawaii, that we was getting nearly to.

Hawaii was like what everybody has surely seen with their own eyes in the movies. Grass skirts and ukes, and Betty Grable and flowers around the neck, though there wasn't as much of all that now because of Pearl Harbor. We went right by there and it sure looks awful. But war or no war, Hawaii is like you expect, only with more soldiers and sailors.

Herbie and Jimmy had promised me they wouldn't tell people about where all I had been. And they didn't, and so I didn't have to tell about it to everybody.

This was goodbye to both of them, too, because I had to get on another plane to go the rest of the way.

I only had a little bag I'd bought in Australia. In it was a few things I'd had to let the council buy for me, as well as the precious little box I had saved, my little green bug and my book.

So in Hawaii I threw away my lingerie and bought some more. There was no place to wash anything but stockings on the plane, and Herbie's and Jimmy's was a man's plane so I didn't like to leave things around. So I bought some more like I said, and I said goodbye to Jimmy and Herbie.

The other plane was bigger than anything I had ever rode in, and it seemed nearly as far to San Francisco as all the rest because I was worried about Pop and where had they sent Jeff off to fight the war, and where I could get a job. And thinking a lot more about Mattoon, like I always did.

I wondered where Aunt Helga got the idea, as if she'd always wanted to, and why she hadn't done it long before. If she did do it.

And by that time there was San Francisco and California, too. And did my feet itch to get on it.

We landed and got out, and a lot of soldiers around and newspaper men and photographers surrounded me, and I had to pose for 'em.

Well, while I was posing this way and that, and saying "No" to having the skirt "just a little bit higher over the crossed knee, please," somebody in the crowd says, "Hello, Miss Garbo." And my heart stopped. And, "Well," the voice says, "tell us all about your trip," and it was Mr. Wens.

I could have died for joy, and I thought, "He sure keeps up with what goes on around the world to be here to meet me." It didn't occur to me to think that Aunt Mary might have let him know. But Aunt Mary had, so he had.

Mr. Wens said Pop had been pretty sick, and that he knew Jeff had been shipped away but didn't know where.

I told him a lot, and he listened and kept shaking his head, big-eyed and serious about some of the bad things and chuckling about other things. He called me Cinderella and Alice in Wonderland and kid names like that. Then he said we were going to fly to Chicago.

But first we had dinner and went to the theater and then to a place up on a hill where you could see all of San Francisco. And at the table, Mr. Wens says, "How about it, big shot, do you want me to manage your career for you?"

And "What career?" I says.

"Well," says Mr. Wens, "it's no use being modest. You can cash in on all this publicity, and get enough dough to do it all over again, deluxe, when you feel like it."

"What would I have to do?" I says.

"Go in the movies, do a lecture tour, write a book, sell your face to advertise sunburn lotion."

"Listen, Mr. Wens," I says, "all I want is to see my pop and get a job that I'm fitted for and see a few other people that I don't know where they're at yet, and to never see my name or my picture in anything."

"You're wonderful," he says, "and there's only one of you in this world, and, by God, I hope you can fight 'em off and do it. I'll do my best to help you."

So I said I was tired and he took me to the hotel I was sleeping at and up to my door. I had to laugh at what a funny boy he was, saying things nobody else could say in such a way you couldn't think he ought to have said it. Like when we got to the door of my room, he said, "Don't tell me that you've come back

from this little adventure as good a girl as you went."
And after I had laughed at that and put out my hand,
he says, "I was sure right, when I first saw you in that
white number in Mexico City and called you the Snow
Queen. Good night, my little ice maiden." And when
I asked him if he wouldn't like to come in for awhile,
he said, "No, I don't think so, because it wouldn't
mean what I wish to God it did mean. See you
tomorrow at nine, princess," he says, "at which time
we start back to where I can turn you over to your
rightful owner, with seals unbroken, damn it." And he
was gone till the next day.

Boy, I sure was tired, so I quickly had a hot bath and
crawled into a real bed for the first time in I don't
know how long.

I woke up to let in a bellboy with four white orchids
and a card in 'em with Mr. Wens's right name on it but
scratched off—why, I don't know—but on the other
side he had written, "Pure like you, white like you, expensive like you, and only God can make them. Wens."

I wore the orchids down to have breakfast with him
and he showed me papers full of war and me, but I was
so anxious to get started I didn't want to eat hardly, and
certainly not to waste time reading things about myself
that I already knew.

"You're sure you won't disappoint me now by
writing a travel book?" he says.

"I've already written a lot," I says, "but don't worry,
it's just so I can show it to my grandchildren," I says,
"so they won't think I'm lying too bad."

"Let's go," he says, and we did.

It was better flying over the land, and my own land at that, as they say in the songs.

We had fun, with officers and two nice girls that were army nurses with uniforms. They were a lot of fun, and they made me kind of proud that women could be like soldiers and good fellers, and yet know when a joke has gone far enough, and still not be prissy.

Now, just to prove to myself that Mr. Wens wasn't right, and that this is no travel guide, I'll skip everything till we got to Chicago.

The pilot was nice, and before we landed he showed me a pilot's eye view of Chicago. There was the Wrigley Building, and the lake, and Michigan Boulevard, and the Outer Drive and all, just as if it didn't know I had ever been away, and it sure didn't.

Cities don't miss you. There's always plenty of others to take your place, and that made me think of Butch's. I asked Mr. Wens, and he said he hadn't been there, but he had heard Pimples hadn't gotten out of jail. He said we'd go there tonight and see, and then I could get a night's rest at the Drake and start off to Mattoon tomorrow to see Pop.

"I don't know about the Drake," I says. "What money I got left, I better use to pay Mrs. Calahan that I owe some rent to," I says. "And I should get back to my few belongings, if she hasn't sold 'em," I says.

But he only laughed and said, "What a girl," again.

We were coming in to land so I buckled my belt. And as we leaned over forward to come down I'm ashamed to say my old trouble came on me at the sight of Chicago coming up to meet me. I thought those butterflies had

molted into caterpillars and that I had graduated from
them that night at Mulloy's, but no, there they was still
on the job. But they settled down as soon as my feet was
on Illinois.

It didn't seem like I could believe it. Here I was in
Chicago, and maybe none of it had happened to me at
all. I could have been standing there yet wondering, but
then the reporters and photographers came with their
flash bulbs, and that brought me back to life.

So after a picture or two we got in a taxi and drove to
the Drake—the same rooms up near the top. Mr. Wens
told me to telephone Mattoon, on him. I had the receiver
off the hook and the operator had said, "Order, please,"
before I remembered that Aunt Helga didn't have a phone.

So I took a bath and went to sleep for a nap, singing
to myself that old song that starts, "Chee-caw-go, Chee-
caw-go, dum-deedily-dum."

The telephone woke me up—it was Mr. Wens downstairs. I dressed and went down. We drove to Mrs.
Calahan's and did I get a surprise.

Mrs. Calahan was a circus performer before she got
too fat for her brother to catch her. He could still catch
her—she said he never had missed in twenty years—but
her weight was too much for his knees on the trapeze,
so she couldn't do it anymore.

"Well," she says, "come in, come in," and I wondered
what could had come over her. But it seemed like she
had seen the mystery-woman pictures in the papers
because she had saved my things and even washed out
a slip and a pair of knickers and ironed 'em, too. She said
I was a celebrity, and she was glad to have had me in her

house. She only charged me what I owed and no interest, and said she was glad to have me back anytime—or the young gentleman, if he didn't have a place.

Mr. Wens thanked her and told her he was my manager.

Just as we were leaving she says, "By the by," she says, "a lady has been coming here asking to get in touch with you off and on. Gray hair and sad face. I can't just recall her name but a very respectable person."

So we went away, me wondering who it could be. We had dinner and went to a show, and then after midnight we went over to Butch's.

I was glad to have Mr. Wens along, on account of Yanci and the Beaver, or maybe even Pimples.

We went in the door, and I couldn't hardly believe it could be so much the same—Butch behind the bar, a few customers, the juke box lit up and playing, Moe holding a tray like always with both hands flat under it on account of no thumbs. And a girl selling cigarettes, out of a new bright-red tray, her long white formal around the floor. And who was it but Millie.

I just looked and stood there with my mouth open, for here was Millie as slim as I was, pretty near, and her hair newly touched up and done very nice, and all fixed up as if she hadn't never met that Curly.

But just then, she saw me, and she let out a yell that made the customers all turn around. She hugged me with the new tray up, edgeways between us, and the packs of Chesterfields and Old Golds and Luckies went all over the floor.

Moe came over, with his funny way of shaking hands. Even Butch looked pretty near pleased, but not quite—till I asked him if he hadn't found the tray and the cash box, and he hadn't. Nobody had, for there it was, just like I left it, up over the Ladies' john, though now it was covered with dust. Butch counted the money in the cash box before he could really let go and give Mr. Wens a Scotch on the house and me a Coke.

Well, I was scared to ask Millie about the baby, so I says, "Where's Red?"

"He's home," she says.

"You mean you're together again?" I says.

"Why not?" she says.

"Well, that's fine you're together."

"Together?" she says. "Red and me is married," she says, "and being as Red's sprained his ankel at the Y. playing handball, I let him stay home and mind the baby till I get back from work. So you see, it all worked out fine."

"But the baby," I says.

Millie blushed right through that liquid powder she uses to cover her complexion.

"Well," she says, "anybody can make a mistake, I guess."

"Of course, Millie," I says, "and, anyway, Red had forgave your mistake long before I went away."

"I don't mean that mistake," she says. "You sure can get fooled," she says, "and was Red tickled, and did he tease me."

"Wait a minute," I says, "go slow."

"Well," she says, "I guess that Curly, he didn't mean so much to me as what I thought."

"Why?" I says. "Come on, Millie, don't be so ornery, talking riddles."

"You done it," she says. "When I saw your picture in the news," she says, "dressed up all in black and flying off with a man," she says, "I just gave a low moan and doubled up. When I came to I had a six pound premature boy with hair as red as my face was—and that was as red as fire. Well, after that, when Red proposed for my hand," she says, "I just couldn't hardly find any grounds for refusing him," she says. "And that's all."

I thought we were going to lose Mr. Wens, but he got hold of himself after awhile.

All we could find out about Pimples and the others was that they weren't together anymore, anyway they didn't come to Butch's much.

So I was saying goodbye to everybody and explaining to Millie that I didn't want the job back, and anyway, it was hers before it was mine. Then Butch says, "Did you get in touch with that lady who was here a couple of times asking after you?" And he told me about the same as Mrs. Calahan had said.

So we went back to the hotel through the north door by the lake because there were reporters at the other one and in the lobby.

So I slept in the room with the rose-colored curtains. I had plenty to think about, but like always, nothing stops me from getting a good sleep, so I did.

There were more papers full of me that came up with breakfast. Mr. Wens came up, too, and we had breakfast in the parlor. Then we went to the station.

"The last lap," he says as we got in a yellow taxi, that like all yellow taxis, brought a lump in my throat.

"How do you account for your good luck, Miss Universe?" says Mr. Wens.

"I've got a bug," I says.

"Dear, dear," says Mr. Wens.

"Some bugs are good luck," I says, "and I got one of that kind." And I pulled the chain out of the neck of my dress and showed him the green scarab that Mr. Bosco had crossed my palm with on Christmas Day.

"That's the chain the old prince gave me," I says, "and this is a little bug a friend of mine gave me. When I saw that the little bug had a little link on it for hanging, I hung it on, and I wear it for luck. The chain was supposed to be for a pretty big diamond, but I kept that safe in my bag so it got lost. But I must say, if I had to lose something, I'm sure glad it wasn't this bug."

"You mean the diamond got sunk with the plane?" he says. And I told him that it was sunk along with everything else—except the little box that it seemed like something had helped me to save, and that I wasn't going to open till I got home.

"Yes, sir," I says, "that little bug took care of me and always will."

But I didn't say anything about the children and grandchildren Mr. Bosco had said it would bring me, not wanting to remind myself that I didn't know where Jeff was at.

Mr. Wens had said last night that he would try to find out, and somehow, I thought there was nothing Mr. Wens couldn't do. He hadn't found Jeff for me yet, but that morning I still hoped he would.

CHAPTER FIFTEEN

WE GOT TO THE DEPOT and was it crowded. We had quite a wait for my train because I had been so scared of missing it.

While we were standing first on one foot and then on the other, I heard my name, and I looked and saw a little gray-haired woman waving at me over the shoulder of a sailor. She looked familiar, but I couldn't place her.

Even when a porter moved some bags so she could get through I didn't know who she could be. Then she came over and spoke to me and took my hands and big tears spilled down her face.

It felt cold in the depot when I realized who it was. "Why, Mrs. Harwood," I says, and I introduced her to Mr. Wens (that I remembered to call Mr. Swift). He saw that she wanted to talk to me, so he said he wanted to get some magazines, and left us by ourselves, me and Dr. Harwood's wife that my brother had shot so dead.

As soon as Mr. Wens was gone she put her hand on my arm.

And "Listen careful," she says, and she told me she and Dr. Harwood had talked it over, and he was so sure the boy was the guilty one. They had both hated Willie's testimony because he was trying to mix poor Uncle Ulrich up in it.

Well, they didn't have hardly any money, she said, but as the doctor's trial went on, it seemed like her husband had more money. Then she found he had that very expensive lawyer.

All of this had worried her a good deal.

And then when her husband got killed by Willie, she couldn't help wondering how it had happened that her husband was killed in Uncle Ulrich's shop. What was he doing there, she wondered. So the doctor got killed and Willie got sentenced, so she came to Chicago and got a job.

After a year she sent for her furniture and when it came she found in a little drawer in the doctor's desk three letters to her husband from Uncle Ulrich.

The first one said that he would arrange for a lawyer, and that the doctor was to be sure not to forget their agreement. The next two were just notes that had come with checks. One of the checks, for two hundred and fifty dollars, was signed by Uncle Ulrich. It was still in the envelope because her husband hadn't cashed it before he died.

So she just put the check and the letters in a plain envelope and addressed 'em to Aunt Helga in Mattoon and sent 'em off.

Well, the very next week, she read about the inquest on Uncle Ulrich, and started worrying over these things—her letting Aunt Helga know anonyomously that maybe Uncle Ulrich had been guilty about Darlene, the girl that Willie had brought to the doctor and then had died, getting them into all that trouble. And Mrs. Harwood worried over whether they had anything to do with each other. So she had tried to find out where I could be to ask me about all this.

She had seen pictures in the papers saying that I was back and staying at the Drake. She'd gone there and the hotel porter told her he had gotten my ticket to Mattoon on this train.

Now, what she wanted to know was, did I think it could be her fault if anything had happened to Uncle Ulrich?

I knew I had to put the kibosh on what she thought, right now, once and forever.

I always knew when I had to decide something important by that little flutter of butterflies, and I sure felt 'em now. But I leaned over and gave Mrs. Harwood a little hug.

"Listen, Mrs. Harwood," I says. "You're a fine lady," I says, "and you've had more than your share of trouble. And I think it's good you found me, before you got so worried you might do something that would maybe make a lot more trouble for yourself. I'm pretty near the only person that could ease your mind," I says, "so listen careful."

I had to get this settled once and for all, and the decision I had to make wasn't any little decision, I can tell you. But, when I thought what could happen if she went on worrying like this, I knew I had to do anything to stop her, or we'd sure be in the paper again.

So I took a deep breath and I says to myself, "Butterflies, do your stuff, but here goes."

"Listen, Mrs. Harwood," I says, "it never happened, what you think. I was at Uncle Ulrich's inquest, and he died of an old ailment, the doctor said, brought on by eating mushrooms that was always poison to his system."

She opened her watery eyes, and "I see," she says, but I saw I hadn't convinced her yet.

"Listen," I says, "I was with my brother, Willie, over at Springfield the night they did what they did to him, and Mrs. Harwood, that boy broke down and cried and told me Uncle Ulrich had nothing to do with it. He wanted Dr. Harwood to help him put it on Uncle Ulrich but he wouldn't. So Willie made up his mind to get the doctor. He hid in the butcher shop because he had heard Uncle Ulrich on the phone, asking the doctor to come there. And when the doctor came, he did get him."

My butterflies were zooming and looping, but I still had one more lie to say.

Mr. Wens was at the gate now with the gateman, both of 'em yelling and pointing at the tail end of the train, just waiting to pull out.

But I had to finish, so I nodded to him and took her arm and walked her towards the gate.

"I'm sure glad, Mrs. Harwood," I says as we walked and the gateman looked at his watch, "I'm sure glad you didn't do anything that might have hurt poor Aunt Helga more than she had to suffer by poor Uncle Ulrich's death," I says. "She told me," I says, "that she got the letters and that she didn't know, but she had hoped it was that you had sent 'em. She was so touched that you wanted to show her how kind Uncle Ulrich was to other people, just like he always was to her. Now you can forget it all, except that you did a kind deed for another poor widow like yourself."

With tears of gratitude in her eyes, Mrs. Harwood kissed the biggest liar in Illinois. Mr. Wens pushed me on the train while it was going. He stood there on the platform waving, but my butterflies were fluttering so I had to get the porter to open the little door quick, so I didn't get to wave back to Mr. Wens.

I hadn't let Pop or Aunt Helga know I was coming or anything because I didn't know how sick Pop was; I thought I had better just walk in.

The more I thought of me getting home, the more the feeling of me going to see Pop got so big in my chest it nearly pushed out the ache that I wasn't going to see Jeff for I didn't know how long, if ever. But when I thought about Jeff again the feeling about seeing Pop was pushed over to make room for that.

I thought about the lies I had told, that I always thought I was never much good at before. And I thought surely Willie would forgive me. It couldn't hurt him now, and I had learned enough about trials to know that if Mrs. Harwood ever told that coroner about the checks and how she had sent 'em to Aunt Helga, it would all be gone over again.

No, I was glad I had done what I did, and I asked Willie to please forgive me for saying those lies about him.

All this I was thinking while I was sitting for the first time in the parlor car. We were going into the ugliest part of Mattoon, if there is an ugliest part. I felt like Willie would have understood and would have forgiven me if he could. So I stood up and was ready to get off long before I needed to, but I couldn't wait.

"Anyway," I thought, "now I know why Aunt Helga

waited a year to do it to him—if she did do it to him."
I didn't like to think she did but had to.

Mr. Koltinsky took me home in his taxi. He had seen
the papers and he wanted to know a lot, and I talked to
him with my mind shut.

And then we turned the corner past the Passtime
Theater that used to be Mrs. Murphy's Ice Cream place,
and there was the street and the house, with the fence at
the low end of the yard painted new where Pop had filled
the ground in, and there was the porch and the door shut.

I got out and paid Mr. Koltinsky and he said, "Glad
to see you back," and wouldn't take any tip.

I opened the gate that was always easy and firm,
because such a good carpenter lived here. And I put my
hand on the knob of the front door that was always
unlocked, and then I thought, "Suppose it's locked,
suppose nobody lives here, or suppose that something
has happened to somebody." And I got so scared, I didn't
dare to try the door.

So I rang the bell, which I hadn't never done before
in my life, and it sounded like a bell in a house where
somebody had died.

I stood there listening to how fast I was breathing; I
stood there for too long. And then the door opened, and
it was Aunt Helga. And then over her shoulder in the hall
was Pop with his mouth twisting out of shape. Then we
were all hugging each other in the dark hall. I was
hugging Pop and Pop was hugging me, and my hat fell
off. Aunt Helga picked it up and went in the dining
room and shut the door. Pop took me into the parlor and
we sat on the sofa. I put my forehead on his thin old

shoulder till I could feel the buckle of his overall strap pressing into it, and I just sighed and settled down, and I was home.

After a while Aunt Helga came in, looking pretty and sweet, with a big tray of sandwiches and a big pot of tea. Pop made me take off my shoes and he tucked the crocheted quilt around me and sat and looked at me, smiling. While we all drank and ate, I talked and talked and told 'em about everything I could think of.

I told them about the little green bug and showed it to 'em, and told 'em what the wish was about having grandchildren. When I told them what the prince had given me and how he had told me not to open the little gold box till I got home, I could see it began to get pretty exciting for them, especially about it keeping me comfortable all the rest of my life.

Finally I got to the part about us getting shot down, and me saving nothing but the bug around my neck and my writing book and one little box.

They got so interested, and Pop said, "Well, I guess this is the time."

"For what?" I says.

"To open it," he says. "You're home, and I thank God for that, be he Catholic, Lutheran or Indian," he says, "you're home. But it don't seem to be for want of trying to get yourself killed," he says.

So I says, "All right." I opened my bag and there it was, pretty near the only thing I had brought back to prove I'd even been. So I gave it to Pop, and he says, "You better."

And I says, "Oh, no, you better."

And Pop says, "I think you ought to."

And I says, "I would rather you opened it, Pop."

And Pop said, "All right. Podner." And he started to. But just then, I heard something. And it was the sweetest sound ever made in the world since the angels sang in Bethlehem about peace on earth and goodwill to men and all that. It was sweeter than Lily Pons or any other music, and it made my hair curl and uncurl all over my neck. I knew that sound, and the heavens just naturally went crazy with music.

It was the stomp of a big heavy old G.I. boot on the porch, with a big heavy old Texas foot inside of it.

Don't ask me how I knew. I hadn't dared to even ask if they knew where he was at. But there it was, and it shot me up off of that sofa and out into the hall, my stocking feet not hardly touching the floor. I don't know how I knew, but I knew it couldn't be the mailman or a neighbor or Buffalo Bill on a mule, it was Jeff and nobody else. So I opened the door and stood there, waiting, hoping for the cyclone to hit me, but it didn't, not right away.

Jeff just stood there for a long time and he came in quiet and shut the door quiet. He didn't seem able to say or do anything and neither did I. Then he says, soft and hoarse in his throat, "Oh, Jesus," he says, "oh, thank Jesus." And still I couldn't move. And then he began to grin with big tears in his eyes, and "For God's sake," he yells, "what are we waiting for?" And, boy, I sure had forgotten how strong he was, and how big and rough and gentle and everything that I ever wanted in this world or the next.

After about a year, we went into the parlor and sat down, and "Listen, podner," Pop says, "I still got this here little box, but I sure think it's you that ought to open it," he says.

"Go ahead, Pop," I says.

So he opened the box and his forehead wrinkled right up, and he looked like he had opened a bureau drawer to get a handkerchief and found a litter of strange kittens.

"Look," he says, so we did. And then after awhile, "How's this going to make you comfortable the rest of your life?" he says.

"That ain't the box that's supposed to do that," I says. "That box is at the bottom of the Indian Ocean," I says, "along with pearls and emeralds and diamonds and some of the finest people I ever met," I says. "But this is the one I saved," I says, "and if it makes you comfortable for the rest of your life," I says, "that's all me and Jeff care about."

"But hadn't you better give it to Jeff?" Pop says. "Why, there never was such a pipe in the world."

"It ain't mine to give," I says. "It's yours. Look how you're printed on it, in gold. It was sent to you, special, by the Rockefeller of Burma. And besides," I says, "I got something else for Jeff." And I took off the chain from around my neck with the little green jade scarab bug hanging on it and I put it in Jeff's big hand.

"What's this?" he says, sitting there on the sofa and looking down at me.

"It brings good luck," I says, "and makes you have many children and grandchildren," I says.

And Jeff squeezed me tight with one arm around me and his big hand flat on me. And the butterflies flew and flew, but I never felt better in my life.

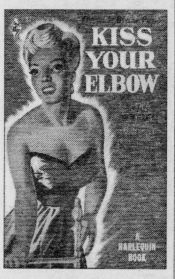